FROM THE NOTEBOOKS OF
MELANIN SUN

FROM THE NOTEBOOKS OF
MELANIN SUN

JACQUELINE WOODSON

THE BLUE SKY PRESS

An Imprint of Scholastic Inc.   New York

The Blue Sky Press

For information regarding permission, please write to:
Permissions Department, The Blue Sky Press,
an imprint of Scholastic Inc.,
555 Broadway, New York, New York 10012.

The Blue Sky Press is a trademark of Scholastic Inc.

Library of Congress Cataloging-in-Publication Data

Woodson, Jacqueline
From the notebooks of Melanin Sun / Jacqueline Woodson
p. cm.
Summary: Thirteen-year-old Melanin Sun's comfortable,
quiet life is shattered when his mother reveals she has fallen
in love with a woman.
ISBN 0-590-45880-9
[1. Mothers and sons — Fiction.
2. Lesbians — Fiction.
3. Afro-Americans — Fiction.]
I. Title.
PZ7.W868Fr 1995
[Fic] — dc20
93-34158 CIP AC

12 11 10 9 8 7 6 5 4 3   6 7 8 9/9 0/0

Designed by Elizabeth B. Parisi
Printed in the U.S.A.   37
First printing, May 1995

Acknowledgments

Thanks again to all of those who stood behind the
dream of this — including Dianne Hess; Anna Grace;
Linda Villarosa; my sisters in Alpha Kappa Alpha;
Michelle Adams; Catherine Saalfield; Alicia Batista;
MaeBush; Marsha and Carole — and everyone else
at the Provincetown Post Office! — and, of course,
the MacDowell Colony — for faith, support, and
time.

For my sister, Odella, and my brothers,
Hope and Roman Woodson,
and for my other family —
Maria, Samuel, Jillian,
and Samantha Ocasio

After John Muir

Today's news is this:
the amphibians are vanishing.
Rice paddie and stomach brooding frogs, gone.
Glass frog, rain frog, golden toad,
Corroboree, toadlet, gone. Yosemite toad.
Tiger salamander, spade foot.
Bufo bufo, so called "common toad."
Cascades, *Tara humare,* Goliath,
Medusa excellus.

It is as if we woke up one morning
and found our mouths missing,
the small wet we relied upon
with inattention.
It is a dream of a world without lily pads
no tadpoles absorbing tails
no eyes afloat on placid ponds.
No witnesses.

But this is it for real:
a world without the single strand
of tapioca eggs
chaining from the underside
of a rare green leaf:
this precarious
this brilliant
this so perfect
as to seem inevitable.

— GERRY GOMEZ PEARLBERG

FROM THE NOTEBOOKS OF
MELANIN SUN

THIS IS BROOKLYN. Summer. Hot like that with a breeze coming across this block every once in a while. Not enough air to cool anybody. Just to let us know we're still alive. A whole city of us — living and kicking. Walk down any Brooklyn street and there we are. Here I am. Alive. If nothing else, Mama says, we have our lives. Who knows what she means by that.

Sometimes, I don't have words. I mean, they're in my head and they're zigzagging around, but there's all this silence in my mouth, all of this air. Maybe people think I'm dumb 'cause I'm kind of quiet and when I do talk, the words come pretty slow. Once they even put me in a slow class, but Mama shot down to that school so fast, the people who had thought up the crazy idea were probably sorry they ever thought anything. Mama says it's okay to be on the quiet side — if quiet means you're listening, watching, taking it all in.

And when I can't speak it, I write it down. I wish I was different. Wish I was taller, smarter, could talk out loud the way I write things down. I wish I didn't always feel like I was on the outside, looking in like a Peeping Tom. I wish I could slam-dunk, maybe break a backboard or two. I wish my name was Donald sometimes, or even Bert or Carlos. Or something real normal, like David. But it isn't. It's Melanin. Melanin Sun. I'm almost fourteen. Five feet ten inches tall. Still growing. Today I'm wearing a striped shirt. Short sleeves. Baggy shorts. Black Pumas with a white stripe. No socks. A baseball cap turned backwards. I have tiny dreads that I keep real neat — you know — keep them nice so the girls keep coming. A pair of shades I bought on St. Mark's Place. Cost me twenty-two dollars, but they keep the sun out. Mama had a small fit talking about how we can't afford twenty-two-dollar shades. Then she tried them on. Checked herself out in the mirror. Checked me out checking her out. "Can I borrow them tonight, Mel?" It's like that in our house.

These are my notebooks. My stories. All the things I can't speak, or try to speak or remember speaking. The stuff I can't say. Secrets. Skeletons. I used to be so afraid someone would find these notebooks and blab everything. But I don't really care anymore. A part of me keeps thinking, *It don't matter.* Maybe not. I figure I should write it all down, though, the way I'd want someone to read it so that it comes from me, not secondhand and stupid. I'm not a regular boy and I'm not slow. I'm on the outside of things. I wish it didn't matter so much. But it does, doesn't it? Difference matters.

So I keep quiet. Watch. And write it all down.

Imagine

Imagine yourself on the corner of a city street. Maybe leaning against the lamppost there, or pausing after leapfrogging over the fire hydrant a few feet away.

Down the block, two girls sit on a third-floor fire escape, their faces pressed into its grating. Still another window, another building, a young-looking woman holds her baby up. She holds tightly to the baby. It's a long way down.

Some of the windows are boarded up. Some are hung with ragged dusty blinds. In the center of the block there is a gap where another building once stood. Flattened cans and broken bottles are strewn over the long grass pushing itself up in the lot. Right up in front, an old couch has been set on fire. Its charred remains are scattered in the lot, spilling over onto the sidewalk. Two stained mattresses have been thrown out, too. Three small kids are jumping on them.

The block grows loud with the sounds of bigger kids returning in groups and pairs, their schoolbags draped carelessly across their shoulders. The girls are laughing and teasing each other. *There's Angie, the girl I'm a little bit in love with.* Hey, Angie, *I want to whisper.* You gave me your number today because it's the last day of school and you want me to give you a call sometime. *"The summer is long,"* you said. *"We should get together."*

Hey, Angie, I'm not like everybody else but you have to have a way to walk in this world so people don't laugh and call you soft. I can't call you right away 'cause people will start talking. But someday . . .

Angie has ribbons braided into her hair. She walks like the world belongs to her. Maybe it does.

The boys are quieter than the girls, their hands shoved deep into the pockets of their oversized jeans. There's me, a couple of steps back from everybody else. Always a bit distant, Mama says. Always a half a step to the left of everybody.

Imagine you could be two places or four or a million. Where would you be? Leaning against the lamp-

*post watching yourself? Trying hard to get a hold
of yourself from all the many places you are when
you're almost fourteen? Where would you be?*

Imagine your mother.

*A woman makes her way slowly up the block.
She is wearing blue pants and a white shirt, wire-
rimmed glasses. A dot of a gold earring shines on the
side of her nostril. The woman's name is Encanta.
Encanta Cedar. EC to her friends.*

Mama to me.

*Mama slows as she nears our building, the third
from the corner, then swings through the gate that
hangs from rusted hinges and makes her way into the
dim hallway. She stops for a moment, just inside,
immersed in the cool, dark quiet. Slowly, from somewhere in the building, the sound of a baby's cry winds
a tinny melody through her quiet. I wonder if that
sound reminds Mama of me years and years ago when
I was no more than a tiny crying bundle wrapped
up in wool.*

"Will he always be so dark?" neighbors nosed.

*When Mama tells me how they always asked her
this, her voice drops down, gets low and steady, like
she's wishing she had had some of the answers she
has now. "I hope so," she would tell them, pulling
me — her baby, her small warm future — closer to
her breasts.*

The story is legend. Mama's legend.

"Melanin," she whispered when the doctor asked her what name should go on the birth certificate. "Melanin Sun."

Mama always talks about the strange look the doctor gave her. About how he shook his small pale head and glanced at his nurse. About how the nurse gave a slight nod as if to say, "Don't worry, Doctor, I'll handle it." Then she turned to Mama and said, "But, Encanta, melanin is pigment — a tint, a stain. Surely you don't want this poor boy moving through this world . . . stained!"

Mama always tells me how she nodded, slowly, waiting long enough after the nurse had spoken to let her know she had heard, then said softly, "Melanin is what makes him so dark, Melanin is what will make him strong. And, Sun, because he looks up at me and I can see the sun right there in the center of him, shining through."

Mama's a bit corny at times. . . .

"But they'll call him Melanin," the nurse warned.

"They'll call him Mel, they'll call him Sun. . . . There'll be a hundred names for him. But he'll know who he is."

Mama climbs the stairs slowly now. Five flights to where the light trickles in from the roof, to where

*the floors soften into rich smooth pine. To where
there is quiet. That's why she chose this apartment.
Not like there was much of a choice because few
people were willing to take a single mom and her
dark baby son into their building.*

*"You planning on staying awhile?" one landlady
asked, cornering Mama in the middle of the apartment she was looking at and pulling my blankets
back to take a good look at me.*

*"I'd like to," Mama said softly, pulling me tighter
to her. She was twenty then.*

*Maybe she was thinking about her own mother —
how she had died the year before of diabetes. How
she had struggled to have Mama and raise her alone
after her husband walked out into the night and
disappeared. "Maybe," Mama whispered to herself,
"I want to do the right thing."*

*"Goodness, don't baby boys grow up to give me
trouble," the landlady declared. "How come he so
dark, anyway? You're brown-skinned."*

*Mama left without explaining. She would wait
until I was old enough to do my own talking. Even
then she didn't speak for me.*

*So many landlords said no to Mama. They wanted
me to have a daddy. They wanted Mama to have a
car. They wanted Mama to be older, to have more
money, nicer clothes, better teeth, straighter hair.*

Even then it was hard. But Mama found this place, stuck at the corner of somebody else's world — a world of first-generation West Indian and Puerto Rican people. A world of akee and pasteles, of salsa and calypso. A world where people minded their own business while minding the business of fifty other people at the same time. She found a top-floor apartment and decided this was as close to heaven as she was ever gonna get. This place nestled at the edge of Prospect Park. Calling itself Flatbush on a good day. Full of noise and music. "Qué día bonita," the old men sing on the first warm day. And I echo them, "What a pretty day." I learned the language of the other people here. "What for yuh wanna be a-doberin she?" The liquid fire of the West Indies. Mrs. Shirley's southern, "Boy I'll go upside your head so hard you gonna wish you was never born." The slow quiet of the old people, seated in folding chairs beneath trees that really aren't more than saplings. "Mmm Mmm Mmm. Now ain't that somethin' else?" My homeboy Sean got the nerve to tell me I'm not bilingual, talking about a little bit of this tongue and a little bit of that one isn't enough to put on a job application. What for da boy wanna say dat?

This block. This apartment at the top. Me and Mama sipping iced tea while the sun pours into the living room, turning us and everything around us gold. This is all anybody needs to be happy.

"Was I a good sleeping baby?" I asked on my fourth birthday. We were sitting in the dark, watching the candles melt down on the chocolate birthday cake. I took a thick scoop of frosting on my finger and missed my mouth. Mama leaned over, wiping my cheeks and chin with a napkin.

"You were the best sleeping baby in the world," she said. "Now make a wish and blow out the candles." I wished for a red fire truck with a working horn, some Tonka cars, a Lego set, a fire hat, and a water gun.

"No guns," Mama said when I opened my presents later. "Never any guns."

But there was a fire truck, a Deluxe Lego Set, some Tonka cars, and a fire hat.

I remember some parts of those good times with Mama. And sometimes, when I'm remembering deep and hard, I start wishing me and Mama could go back to those easy close days when our lives were as simple as chocolate cakes and Lego sets.

Imagine.

Chapter One

IT HAD BEEN POURING ALL WEEK. Some rain had managed to leak past the crumbling wood around the windowsill, puddling in the corners of it. Now the sky was dark and vague.

"What time is it?" I asked Mama, rubbing the sleep from my eyes as I sat down across from her at the kitchen table. It was Thursday morning. Somewhere along the way we had fallen into this routine of me waking up and joining her at the kitchen table, rubbing my eyes and asking what time it was — as though I had someplace important to be. School was out for the summer now and all that was left was hanging with Ralphy, Sean . . . and Mama when she had time.

"Your growing time," Mama said, a smile curving up at the sides of her mouth. Usually

she just told me the time and we left it at that
without all the philosophy.

I stopped rubbing my eyes and stared at her
impatiently but she was looking off, past the
sheets of rain cascading over the windowpane.

The apartment felt damp and cold even
though it was the beginning of July.

After a few minutes, Mama turned away
from the window, took a long sip of coffee,
pulled the sweater she had draped over her
shoulders closed, and put her feet up on the
small cabinet next to the stove. She's always
putting her feet up on something because she
says since her legs are so long, she bumps her
knees against the undersides of tables.

"I boiled some water for you."

I got up and made myself some tea, then sat
down again.

"What growing time?" I asked finally, not
being able to stand the quiet any longer.

Mama looked at me as if I had just spoken
another language. I hated when she was like
this, mixed up and distant. She called this her
"traveling mood." I call it "distracted." Sometimes she just goes off somewhere right in the

middle of a conversation with you and you practically have to scream to get her attention again. I wondered what was so heavy on her mind this morning that was taking her so far away from me. And why there were bags under her eyes on a Thursday morning.

After a moment, she was back, focusing in on me and although I hadn't noticed my stomach was tight, I felt it loosen, relax. She shifted her legs, took another sip of coffee, and sighed. I stared at the tiny gold hoop in her nose. Last summer she let me pierce my ear and gave me her other hoop. Sometimes we just sit across from each other, playing with our rings. It might seem kind of strange to anyone outside of our family — our tiny, tiny family that's only Mama and me — but to us, it's just something we do. Mama says that's what matters — what feels right to us.

I put my elbows on the table and watched her. Outside, thunder clapped hard, then rumbled back into oblivion. For some reason, I started thinking about my father. He and Mama had never been in love. They went on a few dates or something. Then he moved off somewhere and said maybe they could stay in touch

once he settled in a new place. But I guess he
never really settled anywhere because he never
called.

I frowned and thought about how stupid
people can be sometimes. They're always asking me how does it feel not to have a father.
How can I know the answer to that? I don't
have anything to compare it to. It feels the way
it feels. Like if you were born blind. I hate when
people start talking about how they feel sorry
for blind people because they can't see the
beauty of a rainbow or the soft yellows and
grays and browns of new kittens. Like a blind
person's life isn't as good because they don't
have something that other people have. I mean,
how could you miss something you never had?
People are so caught up in trying to force their
own world onto everybody else's that they
don't even get the fact that the other person
doesn't care. It feels like it's been me and Mama
since the beginning. It feels right and whole and
good.

"Do you ever think about Jonathan?" I asked.

Mama laughed. The laughter sounded kind
of nervous but I wondered if I was just imagining.

"Jonathan was a long time ago," Mama said, looking off again.

"But I'm part him," I said. "I mean, he's my father."

"Depends how you define 'father,' doesn't it?"

When she looked at me, she was smiling but there was a lot of sadness behind it. Maybe she was missing him. Maybe I shouldn't have even mentioned it.

"Actually, I have been thinking about him, Mel. I've been thinking about all the men in my life . . . a lot."

"Don't get corny on me, Ma. If you're thinking about getting married, forget it. A couple of dates here and there, but that's it. I'm not going to be calling anybody Daddy." I laughed, thinking about this. "Can you imagine *me* calling someone *Daddy*? That's craziness."

Mama didn't say anything but she wasn't smiling. Then she rose and walked past me into my room, which is off of the kitchen. I kept watching her. Waiting for her to say more. Waiting for her to explain that "growing time" thing. But she just mumbled something about having to get dressed for work and walked on

through the house to her bedroom. If anyone
would have asked about that moment, I would
have said I didn't feel anything. Maybe I didn't.

Our apartment is small. There's a living
room at the front of the house. The next room
is Mama's, so you have to walk through it to
get to the living room and back through it again
to get to my room. Then there's the kitchen
and the bathroom, which falls off of my room
like the bottom of an "L." Sliding doors, made
out of heavy carved wood, separate Mama's
room from the living room where there are so
many plants in the two windows that when the
doors are slid open, it looks as though you've
walked into somebody's jungle. I water them,
feed them, and keep them growing. Mama
pushes them aside sometimes to look out onto
our noisy block. There's a door separating my
room and Mama's but we never close it, except
if I'm studying late at night and don't want to
keep her up or on Saturdays when she likes to
sleep in.

After a moment, I got up and followed Mama
into her bedroom. She had sat down on the
edge of her bed and was leaning forward to

check herself in the full-length mirror on the wall.

"You didn't explain the 'growing time' thing," I said, leaning against the headboard. "Don't keep me hanging."

Mama smiled. "I'm bringing somebody home tonight I want you to meet."

I made a face. "Why do I have to be here for your date?"

"Because this *somebody* is important to me."

"And?"

"And *you're* important to me. So I want the two important people in my life to come together."

"Can't we go to a restaurant?"

Mama smiled again. "Your treat?"

I watched her paint half circles along the bottom part of her eye with black liner. "Don't put that gunk on," I said. "It makes you look old."

"I don't mind looking old. Everybody over thirty looks old to a teenager."

It actually didn't make her look old. It made her eyes look bigger and prettier and made me wonder who was out there so worth impressing.

"Can Ralphael and Sean come?"

"Uh-uh. No friends tonight."

"Please . . ."

Mama looked at me, smiled, and shook her head. "Don't even try it," she said, knowing if I wanted to, I could say please with enough sweetness to make her change her mind.

"This isn't about marriage or anything, is it Ma? 'Cause I'm not walking down anybody's aisle."

Mama laughed nervously again. "I can't get married, Mel. The world doesn't work that way."

I had no idea what she was talking about but I was relieved so I backed off the begging for Sean and Ralphael. Shoot. Let them eat at home for once. Mama didn't bring men home that often. I figured the least I could do was sit down and have a meal with one. After all, Mama's dates never hung around too long. And usually, after one or two dates with the same guy, Mama was ready to move on.

Chapter Two

RALPHAEL AND SEAN came over a little while after Mama left for work and went straight to the refrigerator before coming into my room.

"Man, put those faggot stamps away!" Ralphael said, leaning over my bed to watch me separate land tortoise stamps from baby seals. The stamps had just come in the mail from Greenpeace.

"This is the last one," I said, pressing an elephant seal stamp over its picture in my book. I knew it was faggy to collect stamps but I didn't care. It was something I liked and as long as I didn't start wanting to kiss on Ralphael and Sean, I was okay. A long time ago, I figured out there was two kinds of "faggy." There's the kind that I guess if I thought real hard,

I kind of was. That's the "faggy" that really
isn't super macho and has notebooks to write
stuff down in. Not diaries. Notebooks. Girls
keep diaries. The other kind of "faggy" was
the really messed-up kind. That kind actually
wanted to be with other guys the way I get to
feeling when Angie comes around. That kind
made me want to puke every time I thought
about it — which wasn't a lot.

Sean sat down on the edge of my bed and
eyed my notebooks. "What's those?" he asked.
The three of us had been friends for forever and
they had been coming to my house for forever.
Forever Sean had been asking "what's those?"
every time he saw my notebooks.

"Nothing," I said. This is what I always said.

"We bumped into Angie," Ralphael said. He
smirked. "She wants you to call her sometime."

My stomach jumped. Angie made me feel
dizzy in weird places. When I saw her on the
street, she always smiled all slow and shy. It
was the kind of smile that makes your mouth
dry up on the spot. I checked my pocket
quickly. The ragged piece of paper that she had
written her phone number on was still there. I
still hadn't gotten up the nerve to call her. I had

wanted to talk to Mama about it, but no time ever seemed to be the right time anymore. If she wasn't in class, she was at the gym or at work or out having dinner. Then there were the nights she called to say she wasn't coming home at all. Not like I was scared to be in the house by myself or anything. . . .

"You ever going to call her?" Ralph asked.

I shrugged. "The summer's not over yet."

"Yeah, right!" Sean laughed. "You just don't have the dollars in your pocket it would take to treat her right." He punched me on the arm. Sean was small for his age and a bit mean. His mother and father fought loud and publicly and this must have had something to do with him going off at times for no reason at all. I felt a little bad for him but that wasn't the reason we were friends. We had grown up together, had played Freeze Tag in second grade, baseball in third, and I don't know how many millions of video games together. Hanging with Ralph and Sean was like breathing to me. I couldn't imagine anything else.

"Let's head out," Ralphael said. "Since your refrigerator is so tired-looking, we might as well go grab a slice or something."

I slid the book of stamps into my desk drawer. "I can't hang long," I said. "Mama's bringing some man home for me to meet."

"Tell your mama to bring *me* home," Sean said. "That woman is so fine!"

"Yeah, so what would she want with your ugly butt?" Ralph said. "Melon-head's mom needs a nice older man, like me." Ralph checked himself out in the mirror on my dresser and smiled. He's fifteen, a year older than me and Sean, and the tallest, and, as far as girls think, the best-looking. He's dark like I am, with what Mama says is a nice-shaped head. It's an okay head, I mean, as far as heads go. He has dreads, too. But when you think about it, his head looks a bit like a lightbulb. I guess Mama can't see this.

"Your mama hasn't brought somebody home in a long time," Sean said, leaning back on my bed.

"Yeah, Mel," Ralph said. "What's up with that?"

I flicked the side of his head as I walked past him. "What do you mean, what's up with that? Who am I — the dating game? She's been busy with school or work, or working out. What-ever."

*   *   *

Mama had been spending a lot of time at a health club she had joined in the city. The one time I went with her, I couldn't help noticing how dark she and I seemed among all these white people. I don't have a lot of reason to spend time with white people — they don't live around here or go to my school. I mean, I have white teachers but they're teachers, so they don't really count. Mama must have introduced me to ten women friends of hers and it made me feel a bit strange, like Mama had some secret community I hadn't even known about. I mean, not like I would want to spend time with a bunch of women (I'm not that kind of faggy, either) but it was interesting that she hung with all of these white ladies. There was one sister there and she was a little on the fine side so I spent most of my time trying not to look like I was watching her work out. After she left, I went into the part of the gym that had a pool table and television, got a soda and watched TV until Mama was done exercising. If you ask me, it's a pretty fancy health club. I don't see why Mama needs to spend money on exercising when there's Prospect Park not even five blocks away from us. But she says a lot of lawyers go there and maybe she can network and hook up a good job for after she's done with law school. Whatever.

"Your mama must be going to his house instead of bringing him home," Ralph said. He and Sean started laughing and slapped each other five but I didn't see what was so funny. It was true.

"She's busy working and stuff." I was getting a bit annoyed. So what if Mama had a little something going on the side. It wasn't anything important. She was a grown-up. If she wanted a boyfriend for a little while, it wasn't my business. He'd be gone soon enough. Then it'd be like it was before. Mama and me talking quietly in the kitchen, being close. Being there for each other.

"Remember that one guy," Sean said. "The big one that worked for the airport or something. Man, that was one *ugly* brother."

"I know who you're talking about," Ralphael said. "That guy with the big butt. He was bow-legged, too. Mel, your mother must have gone temporarily blind that day."

"And what about that bright-skinned guy with the cross-eyes?" Sean winced, like he was smelling something that had gone bad.

"He wasn't cross-eyed," I said, defending Mama. "He was an accountant."

"Man, I'm sure that guy's parents had to be walked every day."

"If they didn't chew through their leashes," Sean added.

Ralphael slapped him five then looked at me. I wasn't smiling so they stopped laughing. "We're just busting on you, Mel."

"Hey," I said, shrugging, trying to act like I didn't care.

"So who's the new guy?" Sean asked.

"I don't know. She just said I have to be here. This one must be important or something 'cause she said you guys can't come."

"I didn't want to come anyway," Sean said.

Ralphael leaned against the mantelpiece across from my bed. "You never really had to be home for the other ones. We just all sort of ended up here. Maybe she's going to marry this guy or something."

"Wrong," I said. "She said she's not marrying anyone."

"Yeah, right," Ralphael said. "Fine woman like EC's gonna get snatched up in no time. You just don't want it to happen, that's all. You

better start getting ready, though. Shoot —
I'ma go home and pick out a suit."

"Me, too," Sean said. He looked at Ralph
and they burst out laughing.

Both of them make me sick.

Alone

Some days I wear alone like a coat, like a hood draping from my head that first warm day of spring, like socks bunching up inside my sneakers. Like that.

Alone is how I walk some days, with my hands shoved deep in my pockets, with my head down, walking against the day, into it then out again.

Alone is the taste in my mouth some mornings, like morning breath, like hunger. It's lumpy oatmeal for breakfast when Mama doesn't have time to cook and I still don't know how much oatmeal and water and milk will make it all right. It's Ralphael and Sean, my supposed-to-be homeboys going off without me to catch the new Spike Lee flick in Manhattan, then running up to me in the park where I'm shooting hoops by myself, and having the nerve to tell me all about it. "But why didn't ya'll come get me?" I ask, *and they shrug, say, "We figured you were in your house wanting to be alone."*

Some days alone creeps between my shoulder blades and hollows me out.

Today, alone is a pair of new Calvin Kleins wrapped up in white tissue, folded neat inside a brown box from Macy's. Today, alone is this empty house and a tiny note beside the box: Dear Melanin Sun, I miss you. Love, Ma.

Chapter Three

MAMA WAS IN THE SHOWER singing at the top of her lungs. It was a halfway decent song but she was pretty much ripping it apart. It was almost eight-thirty and her "date" was supposed to have been here a half hour ago. Neither one of them seemed to be in a big hurry, though, since Mama still had the water running and the bozo hadn't even phoned to say he'd be late.

I tapped on the bathroom door. "Never trust a man who comes to a date late and doesn't even call," I yelled over the running water. "Means he doesn't care about you."

Mama turned the water off. "Never trust a son who's full of assumptions," she called back.

"What?"

"I never said anything about a man coming over."

I stood there for a moment feeling stupid, my hands shoved dumbly into the pockets of my pants. I knew I wasn't going crazy and I could have sworn she had said this was a date.

"You mean you made me shower and put on clean clothes and *be here* for some lady friend? And Ralph and Sean couldn't even come?" I stood there waiting for an answer. The silence in between seemed to fill the apartment up.

After a few moments passed, Mama opened the bathroom door and emerged wearing a white T-shirt and jeans, her hair and face still damp. "Yep," she said, pinching my cheek as she passed. "Remember Kristin? She was one of the women I introduced you to at the gym that day. I said she had graduated from my law school the year before."

I followed behind her, relieved but aggravated. "Shoot, Ma, I thought this was the big one." I vaguely remembered a Kristin — I mean I remembered the name but didn't have a clue what she looked like. But if she was that fine sister I had sat there watching, then I was more than glad I had hooked myself up a bit.

The doorbell rang and I jumped up. "I'll get it."

Mama cut me off at the pass. "I'll get it," she said, smiling. "Didn't *we* get eager all of a sudden?" she said over her shoulder.

I sat on the couch and tried to look like it was no big deal. And it really wasn't. Until Mama came back in with Kristin.

"You remember Melanin Sun," Mama said. Kristin smiled and stuck out her hand. I glanced at Mama and saw she was waiting for me to make the right move so I stuck out my hand stiffly and mumbled, "Nice to meet you."

Not only was she not the fine sister. This woman wasn't fine *or* a sister. She was white. White white. Like Breck Shampoo-girl white but with glasses. And those straight white-people teeth you know must have cost her parents a million dollars in dental bills. She had that shimmery white-people hair that has a whole lot of shades of brown and blond running through it and a dimple in one cheek. When I glanced at her face, her eyes were bright and grayish — that scary bright gray that you have to look away from fast or else risk getting stuck trying to figure out how far and deep they go.

Okay — maybe she was a little bit pretty. The worst part, though, was that this Kristin lady was dressed almost exactly like me. We were both wearing blue denim shirts and khakis. Mama looked kind of pleased by the whole thing but I wasn't. I stood there silently, thinking about the gray polo shirt I had almost put on.

Kristin was looking at me like she was trying to see right through me, like she knew me from somewhere. I tried to think of something clever to say to get those eyes away from me, but all I could come up with was a stupid "you look nice" that sent both her and Mama into a fit of laughter.

I excused myself and went to set the table. There had never been a white person in our house. There weren't white people in our world. That was it. In a nutshell and hung out to dry. No use for them in this neighborhood. This was *our* place — people of color together in harmony, away from all of *their* hatred and racism. I didn't dislike white people, I just didn't think of them. For years and years, they had fought hard to stay separate from us, and when we finally said, "Keep your stupid land, we'll find a place of our own," they had to come

over to it and check it out. I didn't care that
Mama and Kristin hung out at the gym and had
gone to the same law school. But Kristin wasn't
a part of us and it bothered me that Mama had
invited her into our world. *How* didn't matter.
I wanted to know *why*.

Kristin moved around the kitchen helping
Mama as though our house was her second
home. I didn't have a clue why she seemed so
comfortable here, or how she knew where
everything was. And I wondered if Mama had
really done *that* much talking about this place.
I mean, it's a nice apartment and all, but did
she go and describe every nook and cranny of
it to this woman?

There was something about the two of them
together that made my stomach hollow out, but
again, I couldn't figure out what it was.

I stood at the edge of the kitchen watching
them silently. Every time Kristin said something even the tiniest bit funny (and she wasn't
that funny), Mama threw her head back and
laughed. I wanted to tell Mama to stop Uncle
Tomming the woman 'cause she really wasn't
that funny. *I* wanted to make Mama laugh like
that.

"Put this on the table, Mel," Mama said,

handing me the lace tablecloth we used at holidays. I looked at her and she raised an eyebrow at me. "Then *set* it."

"Whatever," I said.

When we finally sat down, I was half starved to death and tore into my cornbread without waiting for either of them. We were having fried chicken, cornbread, potato salad, and collards for dinner. Mama had rushed home from work and cooked up a storm. Soul food. It figured.

". . . and then I get off the train and am standing there and this guy comes up to me to ask directions only he's looking straight down my shirt as he's talking to me," Kristin was saying. She had launched into a long monologue about her train ride over here. I half listened. When she mentioned the part about the man looking down her shirt, my eyes went straight for her chest. She didn't seem to have much worth searching for. When she finished telling the story, she turned to me, and without even taking a breather asked, "Do you like Arrested Development?"

She had caught me off guard. What did she know about Arrested Development, anyway? Of course I liked them. Who didn't? The lead

performer, Speech, wrote all of these great lyr-
ics. "I like Digable Planets better," I said, looking down at my plate.

"I don't believe you," Kristin said.

"You don't have to," I said, shoving a piece
of chicken wing into my mouth.

"You're really beautiful," Kristin said. "I
can't believe how much you two look alike."

Mama coughed and I looked up quickly. Nobody had ever said I was beautiful — well,
maybe Mama, but mothers don't really count.

I looked at Mama as if to say *who is this
woman?* But Kristin was there, staring me dead
in the eye, so I couldn't quite get the expression
I wanted going.

Kristin and Mama tried to keep a conversation going with me, but it fell over itself again
and again because I wasn't that interested in
talking. I just wanted to be able to talk to
Mama, only Mama. I needed to ask her about
Angie. To ask Mama what I should say when
I called. I needed Mama alone.

"What kind of lawyer are you?" I asked Kristin when one of the gaps of silence became un-
bearable. Mama looked at me and smiled.

"The bad kind," Kristin said. "I defend landlords."

"Mama's gonna be the good kind," I said.

"Yeah," Mama said. "Watch us get to court and be opposing each other."

Kristin smiled. "It won't be the first time."

When Mama returned the look, her eyes held something unfamiliar. I didn't like whatever it was. If she was worrying about court, I wanted to say everything would be all right. But she also seemed happier than she had been in a long time. I sat up straighter in my chair.

Kristin had brought her briefcase over to the table with her, and now she took some papers out from it. "Speaking of bad lawyers . . ." she began.

Kristin looked at me for a long time without saying anything. After a moment, I got so uncomfortable the bottom of my feet started itching. When Mama got up to get some more greens, Kristin said, "You and me are probably a lot more alike than just the fact that we put on the same outfit." She was smiling when she said this but I shook my head. I wanted to say *I really don't think so* but she was Mama's friend and she was just visiting. Soon, she'd be gone, so I decided to get both me and Mama through this moment with very little embarrassment.

When Mama came back to the table, I glanced

at Kristin's plate. She didn't like collard greens.
They sat in a small green pile in one corner of
her plate. Her potato salad had remained un-
touched, also, but now she put a forkful in her
mouth. She didn't eat like us, taking a bite of
this and a bite of that until everything was gone.
Kristin ate things separately. First the chicken,
then the cornbread, now the potato salad.
Maybe she would get to the collards after all.
I wondered if this was a white thing.

Kristin handed Mama the papers she had
taken from her briefcase, and they drifted into
law talk. I only half-listened, glancing at the
clock behind Mama's head from time to time.
Maybe that was why Kristin was here. Since
she was already a lawyer, maybe she had some
friends that would help Mama get a job. Soon
this evening would be over, and I'd have Mama
to myself again. When I realized this, I could
have slapped myself for being so stupid. Of
course that was it. What else could it be?

Tick, tick, tick. Soon. Soon. Soon.

Angie

Angie. Angie. Angie. Think her name all through dinner when your mama's guest is acting like she's never gonna leave. Let the name take you up and away from the table until you're nowhere . . . and everywhere at once. Say her name slow, it's like angels crossing in front of you. Sleep, sleep, sleep and dream of kissing her, of calling her, of showing her your stamps and hearing her say, "This is the one missing from my collection." And for the quickest moment — there's a connection. This is what love is. Easy words coming soft and slow and finding out you're the same person all the way deep inside of yourselves where it matters the most. Angie. Angie. Angie. Say her name soft and her millions of braids are trailing behind her *as she walks slow towards you saying, "Mel. You been on my mind." Make it sugary and sweet. Make it low as a moan, deep as a holler. Angie. Angie. Angie.*

Chapter Four

A WEEK WENT BY with no mention of Mama's friend, Kristin. Maybe Mama had realized she'd done all she could to land a good job and now it was out of her hands. She seemed to be home a bit more, which gave us more time to talk about stuff. But there was something strange about us together these days. Something missing. . . . I had a million questions I needed to ask her about Angie. But every time I looked at Mama, it felt like I was looking at her through layers and layers of something. It seemed more and more we were talking around stuff rather than getting to the heart of things.

Something needed to happen, though. Here I was, going on fourteen, never had a girlfriend. But I had a cute girl's number in the pocket of my jeans and I was afraid to call her. Every time I changed pants, I transferred the number, and because I was always touching it, the numbers had begun to fade a bit and the paper was starting to fray around the edges.

This morning, Ralph had suggested I call her up and ask her if she wanted to come over and check out my endangered species stamp collection. He had said that that was subtle enough and she was probably into stamps and stuff. I was thinking this would be a good idea, but when I turned around Sean was rolled up in a ball on my bed trying hard as he could not to laugh out loud.

"Well," Ralph said. "*I* thought it was a cool idea."

And for a moment, I tried to make believe it didn't matter what anyone thought. But it did. No matter how stupid people acted sometimes, it mattered. A lot. *Stupid, stupid Sean. Stupid, stupid world.*

Chapter Five

MAMA CAME INTO MY ROOM early one Saturday morning wearing this perfume oil called "Rain." The scent of it wafted into my dream. I could feel her gently shaking me. Halfway between sleep and wake, I climbed up a tree to save the last Malayan flying frog. Far off, I could hear Sean laughing and yelling at me to bring my crazy behind down.

"Wake up," Mama whispered. I opened my eyes slowly, feeling the frog taking a final leap out from beneath my fingertips. Almost awake, I felt my hand close over air.

Outside my window, the sky was dawn-lavender, shot through with the dark shadows of other buildings. When I sat up, I could see the black pools of single-story roofs below me.

"Beach day," Mama reminded me. "Supposed to get up to 85, which probably means 90."

"Mama?" She was standing in the doorway now, dressed in a pair of shorts, a polo shirt, and brown leather sandals. Her hair was messy and wet. "The way the sky looks, Ma? You see it?"

Mama smiled and came back over to my bed. She stared out at the dawn for a long time before she nodded. "I want to keep the day just like this," I said. "I want to hold on to it."

"Can't keep a day, Mel," Mama said, her voice hopeful and full of some sort of longing. "A day turns into night just as quickly as it dawns."

"I want this day to be different from other days. Just full up with those colors. I wish . . ." My voice cracked and I caught Mama trying to hide a smile. It was changing. Slowly, it was going from being little boy high to something between a boy's and a man's. Now it couldn't make up its mind.

Mama put her arm around my shoulder. For a moment we stared out the window together this way, just watching the dawn move up over the buildings.

"I wish some things could just go on like this," I said.

"Oh, Mel," Mama said. She rubbed my cheek before moving back over to the door.

"Mama . . . ?"

I didn't know what I was going to say next but I didn't want her to leave. She turned. Rays of light filtering through the blinds cast hazy bluish blades across her shoulders and chest.

"Huh?"

Ralphael's mother doesn't allow anyone to use "huh" in her house. Every time someone calls out to us, we have to say "Yes?" even if we don't know why they're calling us. Even if it's something we want to say "no" to. Sometimes I make fun of Mama, saying, "The way you say 'huh' sounds like someone who's never seen the inside of a schoolhouse, let alone a college." But Mama went to college. Four years while I was growing up. Even now, she has her law school books spread out over the coffee table most of the time, word processing during the day, taking classes at night. She says she's going to be a lawyer but I see her teaching law somewhere, standing in front of a classroom of college kids all waiting impatiently for her to speak — like parents leaning over their first-born's crib hoping the baby will *goo* or *gaa* or just smile up at them.

"There's this girl . . . Angie." I looked up quickly to see if Mama was smirking. She wasn't. Her arms were folded across her chest and she was all ears. "She gave me her number . . ."

"Call her," Mama said before I could even finish.

"I don't know what to say. I never called a girl before . . . just because I liked her." I looked down at my hands, feeling my face get hot.

"Say, 'Hi Angie. What are you up to?' "

Mama was making it sound so simple, I felt stupid even asking her about this.

"That's corny."

"You haven't even tried it. You want me to listen on the other end?"

I looked up quickly. She couldn't be serious. But of course, standing there, looking concerned, she was.

"Of course not, Ma. That would be so lame. How about, 'Yo Angie. It's Mel. What's up?' "

Mama thought for a moment. "What if she says, 'Nothing. What's up with you?' "

I hadn't thought about that. I was going

blank. What would I say? Frogs. Salamanders. Star tortoises. Ugh.

Mama smiled. "Be yourself, Mel."

"You sound like someone's mother," I said.

She blew me a kiss, told me to hurry up and dress, then turned to leave.

"Mama . . ." I said again.

When she turned, I shrugged. "I was just calling to hear myself call you." I couldn't help thinking about that part in *Winnie the Pooh* when Piglet calls Pooh, and when Pooh answers, Piglet says, *"Nothing. I just wanted to be sure of you."* Sean would call these "faggot" thoughts. He thinks I could use a little toughening up around the edges. The hell with toughening up.

"Hurry up," Mama said. "I want to get there before it gets too hot."

Last year Mama bought a used Chevy off of a co-worker and even though it ran well, something was always breaking in it. The air-conditioning had broken the month before, so we drove with the windows down, the warm air rushing against my hand when I stuck it out of the car. Other cars blasted past us, their windows closed tight to keep the cool air inside. We drove past a huge digital clock and thermometer on the side of a building. Eight-thirty. Eighty-eight degrees. Already, there were tons of people in the streets, trying to figure out how to stay cool. Old men sold shaved ice with flavored syrup and plastic bags of wilted cotton candy. At a red light, a man ran up to our car, offering us a set of kitchen knives, cheap. Brooklyn was steamy, gray-green, and loud. I lay back and dozed. When I woke up, a long time must have passed because the gray-green had turned to mostly green and all the people selling stuff had disappeared. Already, I could smell the ocean.

By the time we got to Jones Beach, it was ten-thirty and the beach was crowded. Mama took off her sandals the minute our feet touched the sand and carried them as we walked past the crowds, searching for a place to put our blanket.

"How 'bout here?" I asked.

Mama was looking out over the water absently. She was in one of her distant moods again. I rolled my eyes.

"Here, Mama?" I asked again, a little louder.

She looked around slowly, then nodded. "Yeah, this is fine."

We spread the blanket out and Mama lay back on it, pulling her earphones from her bag.

"I think I'm gonna walk some," I said, picking up my notebook. This one had a loop on the side for a pen. I took the cap off the pen and drew a tiny line on my hand. It skipped a little but seemed okay.

"Be careful."

"What could happen to me on a beach?" I asked, moving backwards away from her.

Mama winked at me. "Anything," she said, smiling, then lay back on the blanket, her head moving slightly to the music.

I turned away from her and continued down the beach, walking along the edge of the water so that it lapped up against my ankles. A group of small kids were building a sopping sandcastle. A tiny blond girl held a cup into the ocean, then ran back over to the group with it.

Taking a look around, I realized again what I always realized when I came to the beach — that no one was as dark as me. Once, walking along here, I passed a bunch of white boys heading in the opposite direction. When I was only a few feet past them, one boy said, "Hey, it's getting mighty dark around here." And the other guys laughed so hard, you'd have thought that was the funniest joke they'd ever heard. White boys sure are stupid. At first, I didn't know what they were talking about, but as I walked, it became more clear. They had been talking about me. I felt stupid then, dark and ugly. Alone. It made me hate white people in a way I hadn't thought about hating them before. It was before my notebooks, before I had a place to write stuff down — get it out of me.

"I would've messed those white boys up," Ralphael had said when I told him and Sean what had happened.

"No you wouldn't have," Sean said quietly. "You would have kept on walking just like Mel did."

We got all quiet then because we knew it was true. If it happened all over again — five or six white boys on a mostly white beach and one sorry black kid — we wouldn't have said anything. Simple. We would have been outnumbered. Outnumbered and mute as glass.

But the amount of hate seemed to have more power to it than anything else. And that's what we held on to when people got ugly with us. The hate — it's like it kept us whole. But it's not the kind of hate you wear on the outside. That would just make us go crazy. It's the inside kind, that sinks so deep you can forget about it until something comes along.

Walking along the beach now, I checked out the scene. It seemed too quiet, as though something was waiting around the edge of the day to happen. Kristin popped into my head. When she was leaving that night, she had said, *"I like who you are, Mel. I really like you."* I didn't say anything. *You have no idea who I am,* I should have said.

A kid was crying somewhere. And further off, I could hear seagulls calling out over the ocean. A spray of salty air washed across my face. A man was fishing off a pile of graffitied boulders. I climbed up a few feet away from him, sat down, and started to write.

Beaches

Mama's lying on a blue-gray blanket, tuned out to everything but the sun. I can't see her. She's too far away. The distance between us is a strange feeling. New. Like maybe me and Mama are drifting. . . . It's hard to talk about it. Hard even to write about.

This is Jones Beach. I've never been to a beach with no litter. We step over it here and keep walking. A girl in a red bathing suit is plunging into the water and her scream lifts up. I wish I had the words for things. I wish I could knock people's socks off by saying clever stuff. But all I can do is talk to Mama. And write stuff down. And it seems more and more, I'm only writing stuff down.

A man with a fishing pole is casting off now. I've never been fishing. Mama doesn't fish. We buy porgies three pounds for five dollars and fry them up. I wonder if you could catch porgies here. Probably couldn't catch anything that wasn't filled with red tide, or some other toxic strain of pollution. I wouldn't eat anything out of this water.

Hey Notebook! No wonder the amphibians are vanishing.

Chapter Six

WHEN I GOT BACK to the blanket, Mama was chomping on a chicken sandwich. I reached into her bag and got one.

"There's some bottled water on the side," she said. "How'd your walk go?"

"Good. I wrote some."

Mama smiled. "Are you ever going to let me read anything in those notebooks?"

I shook my head. "Maybe when I die."

Mama rolled her eyes.

"It's not for you, Mama. It's for me. The stuff I write down is about *my* life."

"All thirteen years of it, huh?"

"Almost fourteen," I said.

Mama looked thoughtful. "I remember when it used to be *our* life." She looked sad when she said this. "It seems like a long time ago."

"C'mon, Ma. It's still our life. Look, we're here together, right? And you keep stuff from me, don't you? I mean I don't know *everything* about you." I took a bite of my sandwich and watched this look creep across Mama's face. Vague and distant. "What's wrong?"

She shook her head. "Nothing. Just thinking." She took a long swallow of water and looked out over the beach. "I wish we had a house on the beach," she said.

"If you get one of those bad high-paying corporate law jobs . . ." I said.

Mama shook her head. "I guess there's no harm in wishing."

"Whoever gets rich first," I said, "has to get the other a beach house."

Mama stuck out her hand and we shook on it. Then we lay back, the tops of our heads touching, and Mama hummed me to sleep.

It was starting to get dark when we finally packed up and left. Mama was silent for a long time on the way home and I thought maybe she was just thinking about work so I didn't say much about anything.

"It was a nice day, Ma. Thanks for waking me up."

She smiled. We were on the Long Island Expressway heading toward the Brooklyn Queens Expressway. Mama concentrated on weaving in front of a guy who had been cutting her off for the past half hour.

"It was nice, huh?"

We lapsed into silence for a while.

"Melanin Sun," Mama said, after a long time had passed. When she called my name, I couldn't remember what I was thinking about but I'm sure it was something important. There is a sand crab that's dying off because of people letting their dogs dump on the beach. I might have been thinking about finding one and digging a hole so that it could burrow deeper, away from the dogs, away from the crowds.

"Huh?" We passed an accident and I leaned past Mama's shoulders to see. A truck with "Wise" written on its side was stranded on the island separating east- and westbound traffic.

Once, on our way to do Thanksgiving with some buppie friends of Mama's in East Hampton, our car spun three hundred and sixty degrees. It had snowed through the night and the next morning it was still snowing. Even though

Mama had been driving carefully, the car still skidded and spun out, spewing snow up past the windows on all four sides of the car. Mama and I ended up in the middle of the divider. It took a while before we could figure out which direction we had been heading. I was more shaken up than Mama but when I looked at her, it was as if I could read her mind and it was saying *I'm so happy you're okay.* Leaning past her now, I grazed her shoulder with my own. It was my way of hugging her, of saying *I'm glad you're alive, too, Mama.*

When I leaned back, Mama glanced over at me. "Your friends ever talk about . . . gay people?"

"What? Faggots?" *I'm not a faggot,* I wanted to say.

"I don't like that word, Mel."

I swallowed. I wanted to explain my faggot theory to her. I wanted to let her know she didn't have to worry about me, that just 'cause I liked collecting stamps and stuff I wasn't going to be one of the *real* faggots. After all, there was Angie, wasn't there?

"Sometimes Ralphael gets all bent out of shape about me caring about extinction and

stuff. Then he says . . . you know, that maybe
I should think about doing stuff that's not . . .
faggot stuff. But I know he's only kidding.
That's about how close we get to talking
about . . . gay people. Why?"

"Do you know any?"

"I don't really think about them much."

"Ummmm . . ." Mama nodded. I couldn't
tell what she was thinking. Her face was all
closed in a way she has of doing when she
doesn't want me to try to read her thoughts.

"How come you're asking?" The minute I
got home, I'd call Angie. Mama didn't have to
worry — I was going to grow up normal —
maybe even have a wife and a couple of kids
some day.

"What about in school? What happens
there?"

"We *learn*. What do you mean what *happens*
there? You went to school." I laughed but when
I looked at Mama, her face was so serious, I
stopped laughing as quickly as I started. "Ma,
you don't have to worry about me, okay? I'm
not gonna turn gay on you. There's a trillion boys
that still hang with their mothers and — "

Mama looked stunned a moment. Then she

started laughing. It was that pretty laugh, which she doesn't use a lot. I felt myself smiling.

She laughed a bit longer, then checked her rearview mirror and changed lanes, still smiling. We didn't say anything for a while. "I'm not thinking you might be gay, honey. That never even crossed my mind. I mean, if you were, I wouldn't — "

"But I'm *not*, Ma. So you don't have to worry."

"But I'm not wor — okay. Let me start again. Does the topic of queerness . . . ?"

"Queerness?"

"Queerness."

"How come you can say . . . *queer*-ness and I can't say fag — "

Mama glanced at me, then stared straight ahead again. "Because when you say the f-word, it sounds like you're spitting. It sounds like you have so much hate."

"I don't, though, Ma. That's just the word people use." I felt my eyes begin to fill up. I didn't hate anybody. I didn't even care. I hated when she picked on me.

Mama reached over and stroked the side of my face.

"How come it has to matter?" I asked.

"I want to know if the subject is talked about. And how?" Mama continued. "Is it talked about? Are there gay teachers at school?"

"Why would I even *care* about them? Why do you? I mean, no one's there trying to teach me to be . . . a queer."

Mama looked at me. "I care because they're people, Melanin Sun. Because I've raised you to care."

There is a bird dying off in the Galápagos that came to my head suddenly. It's called a perot. A man goes from nest to nest checking on the eggs because rats eat them. They're trapping the rats now and they think maybe the bird won't become extinct after all. This was what I cared about, what I wondered about. How God could make something beautiful as a bird, then create rats that kill it off.

Mama's voice faded back in and for a second I thought I wasn't hearing her right. She had pulled the car over to the shoulder, turned the ignition off, and looked at me.

"I need to tell you I'm in love, Mel," she said softly. "I'm in love with Kristin."

Swimming

This is one of those stories that leaves you floating like this book I read about this white guy named Jack. Only this is real life and I'm not a white boy. But Jack's dad takes him out on a boat to the middle of a lake. You knew something was going to happen just by the way the dad was paddling so hard. And when they were smack in the middle, the dad stops paddling and they just sit there for a while. Then the dad lays the news on Jack — that he's queer. And Jack is stuck with this big chunk of info and no way back to shore. Just sitting there, in a boat with his queer father. But there's no lake in this picture, just me and Mama and miles and miles. . . . Still, it feels like I have to keep swimming. Swimming with no shore in sight. No nothing except me and these notebooks. My stacks and stacks of notebooks.

And writing it all down is my way of swimming, of trying to keep my head above water. If you look way out next time you're at the beach, maybe you'll see me, a boy, bobbing and gasping, then going under.

Chapter Seven

I FELT THE AIR LEAVING MY LUNGS, breath by tiny breath until there was nothing.

"No, Mama," I whispered, letting her pull me close. I couldn't stand having her touch me but if she wasn't holding me then who would I be? Where would I be? Alone. Almost fourteen and alone. No mother. No father. No nobody.

I pulled away from her and wiped my nose with my hand. "Take me home," I said, not looking at her.

"Mel . . ."

"Take me home. Now! Take me home." I was screaming.

Mama sniffed, and slowly pulled the car back into traffic. We were silent on the drive home. I stole a look at Mama, feeling something melting away from me. Her face was tight as a fist. I had never seen it like that, so full of pain and something that looked like anger. Swallowing, I thought, *If she touched me, her touch would burn.*

If she was a dyke, then what did that make me? *I'm not a faggot. I'm not a faggot! I'm not a faggot! I'm not a faggot! I'mnotafaggotnotafaggot!!* I wanted to scream this into the tight space of our car. I wanted to run out onto the middle of the B.Q.E. and get hit by the biggest thing coming.

Mama put her hand on my shoulder. "Don't touch me!" I said, jerking away. "Don't ever touch me again."

Then Mama drove. Silently. Miserably. Tears streaming but no sound. We could have been two strangers in the middle of the ocean, a faggot father and his son in the deepest part of the lake. And our boat had sprung a leak. And now it was sinking. Sinking.

When she pulled up to the curb in front of our house, I bounded from the car before it even came to a full stop.

Upstairs, not knowing what else to do, I started punching the walls, hard as I could until holes opened up. I couldn't breathe. I was crying so hard I couldn't breathe. After a few punches, my knuckles started to burn and bleed. It felt good almost. Like I was really alive.

Behind me, I heard Mama telling me to stop punching the walls, stop putting holes in the walls. But our house was filled with holes now and she'd put the biggest one right through the roof — a big giant hole that let in all of this darkness. Even in the daylight, darkness was coming right through our roof and she had the nerve to say, "Stop punching holes." Holding on to my arms, trying to hold me back or up because I felt like I was going to fall right over every time I thought about what it meant that she's a dyke — a big bulldagger who kisses on other women.

"A dyke!" I was screaming this right into her face because she was holding me so close I could feel her breath and she was crying like I'd never seen her cry before. I hated her so so much. I hated that I wanted to hold her. I hated her for being my mother and my friend.

"Melanin, don't . . ." Her voice was soft and broken. I wanted to wipe away the tears and punch her full in the face for ruining my life like this.

"You're a dyke! A dyke! A dyke! You and that stupid white lady. Nobody wants you. Nobody. That's why my father disappeared and even the ugly guys didn't come back. Nobody." My words were hot and loud right in her face like tiny knives being thrown one right after the other, right into her eyes and instead of blood, there were tears.

"Melanin, listen. You have to listen. You have to understand." Tiny fragments of words, sentences I didn't want to hear but she was holding tight to my wrists so I couldn't break away.

"Let me go, Mama! Just let me go!" But at the same time I was falling right onto her chest and blubbering like a baby because I knew everybody was going to know. Everyone. Then I was begging her, crying and begging, "Please Mama. Please Mama be anything. But *please* don't be a dyke."

Chapter Eight

KRISTIN CALLED at eight o'clock that night. I could tell it was her by her voice, all high and breathy and white. When she asked to speak to Mama, I told her to hold on. Then I hung up.

I dialed Angie's number. I was so angry, I couldn't even feel myself being scared. But as soon as a woman answered, I hung up.

A few minutes later, the phone rang again. I let it ring until Mama came out of her bedroom where she'd been since we got back from the beach. Her eyes were puffy. I heard her say, "Hi," her voice melting, then she was unravelling the phone cord and taking the phone into her bedroom, closing the door between us.

I lay back on my bed, put my hands behind my head, and stared up at the ceiling. The dodo couldn't fly. It was easy to catch that bird. Why couldn't it fly? How come its bones were so heavy that it couldn't lift off, away from predators? I wanted to fly, lift off away from everything. Away from dykes.

When I was real little, if you wanted to make somebody mad you'd say something like, "Your mama wears combat boots." And maybe that person would want to kick your behind. I never knew why that made a person so mad, just because his mother preferred certain kinds of shoes. I was dumb as a tree trunk when I was little. Dumb. Dumb. Dumb.

I wish everybody's mother was a dyke.

I heard Mama murmuring softly to that Kristin woman. Then I heard her laugh. Kristin makes her laugh, I guess. I heard her say *This is going to be hard* and I felt my own self getting hard. Stupid, stupid me. It hurts sometimes when I get hard, like I'm going to explode down there. Angie. I think about her sometimes when I'm, you know. Her chest is pretty big. My thing started pushing against my bathing trunks. I tried to stop thinking about Angie's breasts. Ralphael flashed across my brain. Stupid, stupid Ralphael. How come I'm thinking about him? *Faggot. Angie. Angie. Angie. Mama and Kristin. Angie.* If only my tongue hadn't gotten all thick when that woman answered, maybe I'd be on my way over there now. Never even kissed a girl. I heard Mama cough and I moved my thing so that it no longer made my bathing trunks stick out. Girls can hide it. Sometimes, at lunch or something, I'll get a hard-on and I can't hide it. It feels like everybody is looking at it. I try to think about stuff that'll make it go away. Sometimes I think about birds. Sometimes I think about the homework I didn't do and the teacher that's going to scream holy murder because I didn't do it. That usually makes it go away. In the future, I'll probably think of this day with Mama and how she tried to ruin the rest of my life.

I watched the sun go down. First it ducked behind a cloud, then it came back out again. The house was growing dark. Mama was still talking to Kristin. I thought about getting up and making some dinner, then changed my mind. My stomach was filled up with something already. I didn't know what that something was, but it felt like it was all over me, filling me and crawling on me and making me itch. I heard Mama sniff. Then she coughed and sniffed again. I heard her say *I love you,* and something inside of me shut down, went stone-cold. Goose bumps broke out over my arms and legs. I shivered, climbed to my knees, and pressed my head against the windowpane. Maybe Mama hated men. Maybe she hated me.

People say Ms. Brown, the girls' gym teacher, is a dyke. She wears running clothes all the time and her hair is pretty short. She kind of looks like a guy, if you ask me, which makes me think Mama is different. She doesn't look anything like Ms. Brown. Mama's pretty. She was making a mistake about Kristin. They were just friends, that's all. And maybe 'cause she hadn't had a good friend in a long time, she got it all confused.

The sun moved a little, then dropped, and the sky went all orange before it faded. Then all the shadows that had been dancing on my wall melted into a big gray one. I heard Mama moving around and I knew she was in there getting ready for bed. I climbed under the sheet and closed my eyes. Maybe I'd wake up tomorrow and this would be a dumb dream. Maybe it never really happened like this.

Mama, I wanted to say. *Can you please open your door so we can be a family again?*

Sound

It's raining again. Seems like it's been raining every day since that day on the beach. That was two weeks ago. Seems like . . . like yesterday.

EC just left. These days she just says, "I'll be back, later." Then she is gone. And the sound of the door closing — it's like the sound of somebody getting punched hard in the stomach — and then the house is empty and airless.

I'm scared the whole world's going to know. Maybe it already does.

Yesterday, I was in the park shooting hoops by myself, in the empty park, in the rain, not even counting. Listening to the sound of the wet ball hitting the backboard, bouncing down on the wet pavement. And the squishing of my sneakers. All that mattered yesterday was sound, all the different kinds I could make. Sound. Even silence has a sound. It makes me think of how it must be to be dead, in a closed-in, airless, satin-lined coffin with your hands folded across a bible and a cross on your chest.

Everybody but me and Mama died before I was born. That's what she tells me. Grandfathers and uncles and aunts, all gone. What if she dies a dyke?

What if a fire happens and all my notebooks burn? Then what will I have? Lots and lots and lots of silence. Nobody knowing that I ever was.

I feel like my heart is broken.

Chapter Nine

O N SATURDAY, Mama left the house early, without so much as saying good-bye. I lay in bed with my hands behind my head, staring up at the ceiling until her footsteps faded down the stairs. It was raining again. In the distance, I could hear thunder rolling low.

In the bathroom, I left the lights off, stepping into the shower in the darkness. A thin stream of gray light filtered in through the tiny window above the bathtub. After a while, I could begin to see the outline of my arms. They seemed skinnier.

I dressed quickly and left the house. It was too empty in there these days. All the silence was beginning to make me nauseous.

For once, the street was empty as though the rain had scared everyone, even the women forever in their windows, back inside. I walked slowly. At the corner, a slug that someone had sprinkled with salt was writhing. I stepped on it, wanting to put it out of its pain. A drop of rain trickled down my cheek. Maybe it was a tear.

Chapter Ten

L AST NIGHT I DREAMED I was being chased
by this white woman. Only thing is, we
were on bicycles and I was way ahead of her
for a long time. She was pedaling and I was
pedaling and I kept looking over my shoulder
to see how far behind me she was. When she
started catching up, I hopped off my bicycle
and ducked inside this building. Then I had to
pee. I started looking around for a men's room
and instead I found a room with a sign that
said:

BOYS
&
WISHES

I knew it was a bathroom but I was afraid to go inside that one, afraid what I wished for wouldn't come true. Then I saw another sign:

TALL BOYS

Next thing I knew this black kid, couldn't be no less than seven feet tall, walked past me, said, "Excuse me," and ducked into the Tall Boys' room.

So I was standing there, starting to believe in that Boys and Wishes room. Next thing I knew, Mama was shaking me awake and slowly, slowly, the Boys & Wishes room melted away.

"We have to talk," she said, standing above me. Her voice sounded unfamiliar. We had said so little to each other in the past weeks. I was beginning to get used to the silence and her absence, which seemed to be more and more — a couple of times not even coming home the whole night. On those nights, she would call but I'd let the answering machine pick up and keep watching TV until I heard her voice, sounding like a bad recording, on the other end of the line. Then it was okay to fall asleep. I pulled away from her now, halfway between

the dream and being awake. I could feel Mama's
fingers pressing into my bare shoulder. I didn't
want her to be touching me, not now, not ever
again.

"Don't want to talk," I said, pushing myself
against the wall. "Don't have anything to say."

Mama pulled me toward her, making me feel
even smaller. I always forget how strong she
is. Last year, she built a six foot by eight foot
bookcase in the living room. Every book we
own is on those shelves. All kinds of books,
about everything. I wondered if any gay books
were on that shelf and thought of *Zami*, by this
woman named Audre Lorde. I remembered
telling Mama I liked it because the woman grew
up in the city and had gone to the same high
school as me. Now it was dawning on me that
Lorde was a dyke. Duh. Mama must have
known all along. And I had said I *liked* it. Stupid, stupid me. Later on, when Audre Lorde
died, there was a big memorial service for her
at this church called St. John the Divine, and
Mama and I went. There must have been ten
thousand women there. Maybe all of those
women were dykes. I closed my eyes again.
What if? I kept thinking. *What if?*

We used to sit and read a lot, just the two of

us, not saying anything, our heads deep inside of stories about some other body's life. Quiet. Not bothering each other. Sometimes we'd drink tea or lemonade or something while we read. Sometimes Mama would make quesadillas, melting cheese between tortillas and pouring salsa over the top, and we'd sit munching and reading like there wasn't anything else in the world or any other way. You ever hear people talk about how *those were the days*? It's usually old people saying that stuff but when I'm remembering who the two of us were then, I start feeling old. Old and wrinkly and weak like a raisin man.

Mama got up and started pacing. Back and forth, back and forth, like those guys on TV always do when they're waiting for their babies to be born.

"You can't just drop stuff on people," I said. I was half thinking about Mama and half thinking about the boy in the dream. He was so tall. Had he gone into the "Boys and Wishes" room and made a wish to be tall? Was he supposed to be me? Who *am* I, anyway? Who cares?

Mama paced over to the window above my bed and pulled the curtains apart. It was hot again. Rays of sun hit the place on the sheet that covered my feet and I wiggled my toes, feeling them grow warm all of a sudden. My shoulders felt warm, too, even though I wasn't wearing a shirt. I pulled the sheet up over them, not wanting Mama to see. Not wanting her to see any part of me even though she'd seen my shoulders and chest and stomach a hundred thousand times before.

"I've been waiting," Mama began.

I started humming, covering my ears with my hands. I knew this was babyish but I didn't care. What made her think I cared?

Mama swallowed. I watched the motion her throat made and felt my own throat filling up. We used to have such good times. Everybody used to be so happy.

"I've been waiting a long time to be this happy," Mama said. Her voice was so soft, I had to uncover my ears a little bit to hear. I stopped humming and glared at her.

"We were happy."

Mama shook her head. "I have you, Mel. But I need more. I need grown-ups around, people who speak a grown-up language, who've lived a long time. I need friends my age and a lover."

"You think just because Kristin's white, she's

the world. Well she's not. She's just some stupid white lady out to mess with your mind."
I turned away from her and faced the wall.

"Don't give me that white guilt, Mel. We're both smarter than that. Since when did *you* start seeing the world in black and white, anyway?"

"What? You think I've had blinders on for fourteen years? How am I supposed to be in it and see it any other way? I'm gifted, remember? Remember they discovered I wasn't slow after all, that it was the complete opposite? *Gifted*, not *blind*? You think this is about you? Well, it's not."

"Then who is it about?" Mama asked. "Is my life about you now?"

"It's about both of us. Sometimes you act like a stupid little selfish kid. Sometimes I hate to think that you're my mother."

"Well, I am. So you better start thinking it. A lot may change between us, but that won't."

"You should find a man, Ma. The real thing. I guess you can't, huh? I guess no man wants you."

"I guess." Mama said, walking back toward her room. "I guess we have nothing more to talk about."

Chapter Eleven

MAMA COULD PLEAD temporary insanity for thinking I didn't see the world in black and white.

Before Kristin, there weren't tears in our house, just small daily frustrations — the kind that ebb and flow.

One day, before Kristin, Mama came home from a temp job with a bag of clothes a co-worker had given her. The woman, a white lady, told Mama maybe I could use these. She went on to say that she remembered the day she met me and I was dressed in a pair of ragged jeans. Mama told me all of this as she spilled the bag into the bathtub, sprinkled the clothes with torn newspaper, then set them on fire. I couldn't help but wonder, as the small dark pile swelled with smoke and flame, who in the world this white woman thought we were.

Another time, when Sean, Ralph, and I took a hike out of the neighborhood just for the sake of adventure, each and every white woman we passed either clutched her purse or crossed to the other side of the street. *"I feel like snatching her bag,"* Ralphy scowled. *"Just to prove them right."*

Over the years, other frustrations infiltrated. Every television show seemed to feature some black person in jail or committing a crime. Every news show talked about violence in black communities. It got so Mama and I only watched cartoons and corny sitcoms.

I didn't think about white people. They were a different species, living a different life in some other place. At school, where most of the teachers were white, we were indifferent to their color. We didn't think about our teachers' private lives, where they went at night or who they went with, or if they even *had* lives outside of the classrooms. We didn't imagine their pale bodies showering each morning, thin-toothed combs raking through their bone-straight hair. We didn't contemplate what they ate or how they ate it. White, before Kristin, didn't matter at all.

Now it seemed to be everywhere. Kristin and Mama were in every single thought I had. I wondered if they talked about me, planned ways of getting rid of me. I wondered what they did together. How did Mama hold her? What did they see in each other? Why? Why? Why?

Thirteen-Going-on-Fourteen

I am tired now, of being thirteen. Tired of having to figure stuff out by myself. What matters is the people in your life, I think. Who they are and how they treat you. Mama matters. The Mama I used to know. The me I used to know. Now everybody in my life is unfamiliar. My moms pulling the car to the side of the highway to tell me she's queer is unfamiliar.

The world turns upside-down when you are thirteen-going-on-fourteen. I want to ask someone right now — when will it right itself again?

Chapter Twelve

AFTER MAMA LEFT, I got dressed and took a walk to try to clear some of the stupid things that were racing around in my head. Like the minke whale. They've started hunting them again in Norway. The paper says they use them to make cosmetics and candles and stuff like that. It seems like nobody even cares that the world is falling apart. Not just my world, everybody's. People all the time talk about re-cycling this and preserving that, but nobody really cares. I don't think people even think about stuff. Not the people hunting minke whales. Not the rats eating bird eggs. Not Mama.

There's a tortoise — the star-shelled tortoise. It has these beautiful raised diamond shapes on its back. Somewhere in Sri Lanka, it's dying off. Slowly, it seems, everything and every-body and every way that used to be is dying.

"Yo, Melly Mel. Wait up!" I turned. Sean and Ralphael were running toward me, drib-bling a basketball between them.

"Guess who's still asking after your surly butt?" Ralph asked, grinning.

"Who?"

"Angie Baby," Sean sang.

Ralphy shook his head. "You sure can't sing."

"Don't want to be a singer anyway," Sean said. He dribbled the ball through his legs, then swept it up onto his fingers and spun it.

"She's down the block," Ralphael said, pointing over his shoulder. "She's pretty hot for you, Mel. Let's 'bout face and make-believe we were headed in that direction anyway."

I turned and fell into step with them, my heart pounding all the way up in my neck. Then Kristin came into my head — just shot through it like a bullet. What was the use of even giving Angie the eye anymore? It would have been hard enough to call her if things were normal. But now? There was no way I was go-ing to bring her home to my messed-up house.

"What you been up to?" Sean was asking. His voice sounded far away, like it was floating down another block. "Earth calling Melanin Sun," Sean yelled. When I looked at him, he repeated the question.

"Not much," I shrugged.

"Yeah," Ralphael said, squinting down the block. "This has been one boring summer."

"I guess," I said, trying to steady my voice and sound cool. "How you know Angie really likes me?" I asked. I fingered her now-faded number, still on a piece of paper in my pocket. I had memorized it a while back, but I still carried the paper around. For luck.

They both grinned.

"Well," Ralphael began, his voice dropping even though we were still a long way from the group of girls sitting on the stoop at the end of the block, "yesterday, Sean and I were hanging out outside Pancho's and Angie and her posse came by, making-believe they had to buy something."

Sean laughed. "They went inside and came out just as empty-handed. . . ."

"Not even a candy bar or a pack of gum," Ralphael cut in.

"They won't be getting an Oscar anytime soon with that."

They laughed.

"Anyway," Ralphael continued, "they sort of stood there awhile not saying anything, then Angie asks 'Where's Melanin Sun?' She tried to sound all brave and grown up, but I knew she was scared reckless asking."

"What'd you say?" I asked.

Ralphael smirked. "I told her you were around, somewhere."

Yeah, I thought. *Hanging with my queer mother.*

"He said you were probably somewhere sticking harbor seal stamps in a book."

They doubled over, laughing.

"You didn't."

Ralphael bumped my shoulder. "There she is," he said, pointing with his chin.

I scanned the group of girls. Angie looked up and half-smiled at me.

"Oh."

"What do you mean 'oh'?" Ralphael said out of the side of his mouth. "Say something." He shoved me towards her.

I waved at Angie, trying to look cool. I must have dialed her number and hung up twenty times this summer. She has nice teeth — straight and white — and a ponytail of braids with bangs that curl like tiny corkscrews down past her eyebrows.

I took the basketball from Sean and turned. Like two robots, Ralph and Sean turned with me.

"What's up?" Ralph asked.

"Nothing."

"Don't you think she's cute?" Sean took the ball from me and bounced it a couple of times.

"Yeah, she's okay. But I'm not going to talk to her with you all at my shoulder."

We walked back to the corner. The sprinkler was on and a bunch of little kids were running back and forth underneath. I ran my hand through the water, then rubbed my face. The water was cool, soothing.

"You want to shoot a couple hoops?" Sean asked.

I shook my head. "Going back inside."

I heard Sean mumble *homebody*.

"Got some housework to do?" Ralphy grinned.

"Maybe."

"Your mom has you doing all kinds of stuff,"

Sean said. "You won't see me do no house-cleaning. That's what I got sisters for."

Ralphael grabbed the ball from him and dribbled. "Yeah, right! That's why those sisters of yours had you mopping the kitchen last night when you wanted to watch wrestling!"

Sean frowned and stuffed his hands into his pockets. We had stopped at the corner and were looking across the street into the park. Every court seemed to be taken with boys two and three times our size.

"I hate the summer, man!" I said. "Nobody has anything to do but play ball. You can't even *see* the rim until September."

Ralphael dribbled the ball once and shot it through a fire escape rung hanging down about six feet off the sidewalk. The ball sailed through without touching the sides. Sean retrieved it, took the same shot, and missed.

"Yo, Sean, let me try to lower it a little for you," Ralphael laughed. "Maybe I could bring it down about three feet."

Sean gave him the finger and took another shot, missing again. He grabbed the ball after it bounced and came over to where Ralphael and I were leaning against a stop sign.

Mama's car pulled up and she and Kristin got out. I held my breath.

"Hey guys," Mama called, smiling.

"Hey EC," Ralphael and Sean said at the same time.

Kristin waved but none of us waved back. I nodded slightly. She and Mama disappeared into our building and I let my breath go.

"Who's the white woman EC's been hanging with?" Sean asked.

"Friend of hers from law school or something," I said quickly. I snatched the ball from Ralph and dribbled.

"Kind of tasty," Ralphael said.

"If you like white meat," I said, jabbing Ralphael in the side. "Me? I'd be better off with something dark and lovely."

Sean sucked his teeth. "You'd be better off with anything you can get, man!"

We laughed.

"So, Melly, your mama find a boyfriend yet?" Sean nosed. "What about that guy from the other night? Just how ugly was he?"

Maybe they knew already. Maybe the whole stupid world knew. "Very ugly. And dumb? Man, this guy was riding the rough edge of 'vegetable.' You have anyone else in mind for her, Sean? Your father's married. Least that what he's supposed to be!"

Ralphael laughed and slapped me five. I waited for Sean's answer, already knowing what it would be.

"I'm talking about me," he said, brushing off his T-shirt. "Me and your mother would look sweet together!"

I tried to laugh, punching Sean's arm. But the grin on my face felt like it was pasted there, like a bad Halloween mask that might fall right off and reveal the boy underneath.

Sean and I danced around in fighters' stances, jabbing at the air.

"When it turns into a real fight, you two will be sorry!"

All three of us turned in the direction of the voice. Across the street, Mrs. Shirley was leaning out the window on a pillow.

"We're just playing," Sean said. He scowled. "She's so nosey," he whispered without moving his lips.

"Yeah, you playing now. Wait till someone hits somebody like they don't want to be hit. You boys just stop it. No need to be showing yourselves like that!"

"I was just telling them that, Mrs. Shirley,"

Ralph lied. "Just this minute I was saying no need to fight, guys. We're all brothers on this planet."

Mrs. Shirley smiled. "Say 'hi' to your mama, Ralphael."

"I will, Mrs. Shirley."

"I will, Mrs. Shirley," Sean mimicked.

We headed around the corner, out of Mrs. Shirley's sight.

"Nah, man," Ralph said. "That's how you have to be with her. Next thing you know, she'll be all up in my mama's face talking about how we were fighting in the street. And Sean, you know my moms will be over to your house in a quick second. Then, that'll be it for our summer. That's all I need, to be on punishment for the whole summer."

Sean and I nodded. Ralphael had a point — Mrs. Shirley had to be the biggest see-all-know-all on the block. I wondered if she had seen Kristin coming or leaving our house. Probably. Next it would be all over the neighborhood.

We stopped in front of Pancho's. Sean threw the ball to me and ran inside.

Ralphael grinned, throwing his arm over my shoulder. "Mel, you think your moms might be a little bit off the wall? I was just wondering.

Who would name a kid Melanin Sun? I swear, I never *ever* never!"

I jerked away from him, scared all of a sudden. What if Mama and Kristin came back downstairs and were hanging out outside the building? What if they were holding hands or something?

"I gotta go," I said quickly.

Ralph looked puzzled.

"I just got to go," I said again, heading back toward my building. "I'll catch you later."

I got back in time to see them climbing into Kristin's car. When Mama saw me, she got out again.

"Do you want to go for a drive, maybe get some dinner?"

"I got things to do," I said, shaking my head.

"I miss you," Mama said, touching my cheek.

I shrugged. After a few minutes had passed in silence, Mama sighed, touched my cheek again, then climbed back into the car.

Chapter Thirteen

I WAS SITTING at my desk going through my frog stamps when the phone rang a few hours later.

"Can I speak to Melanin Sun?" a girl's voice said.

"This is Mel."

"Well, this is Angie."

"What's up, Angie?" I said, then immediately regretted it. It sounded rehearsed because it was. I had dreamed this moment a million times and now here it was. And *she* was calling *me*. Maybe that made me lame, though, 'cause I should have been the man about it.

Angie laughed nervously.

Breathe, Mel. Start all over. "So what's up?"

"Nothing," Angie said. "I was just calling to say hey."

We were silent for a few moments. I couldn't think of a single thing to say. Stupid.

"Oh, well," Angie said. "I just wanted to say hello. It's hard to talk to you in person since you're always with your friends."

"Sometimes I'm not."

"Like when?"

I thought for a moment. "When I'm in the house."

I looked out the kitchen window. It was cloudy again. Would Angie run screaming from here if she knew about Mama? Would she ever speak to me again? What was the use of even talking to her, I wondered, if the minute she found out, she wouldn't even pick up the phone to dial my number?

"What are you doing?" Angie asked.

"Nothing." *Breathe, Mel. Breathe.* "Collecting stamps and stuff . . . of endangered species. I'm holding one of a Corroboree." *Stupid, stupid me.*

"S'cuse me?"

"Corroboree, bufo bufo, golden toad . . ."

"You sound like a crazy person."

I smiled, embarrassed. She had a nice voice. "Frogs. I know you probably don't think of them as animals. . . ."

"They're amphibians."

"They're vanishing," I said.

"Oh." The line grew silent again. I wondered if Angie was thinking I was crazy. I didn't care. If she didn't like the way I thought about things, she didn't have to call anymore. The heck with her. The heck with everyone.

"I like all the insects and animals and amphibians that are almost extinct or already extinct," I said, kind of giving up on everything.

"Oh," Angie said again. This time it was a different "oh," like maybe she understood a little better. "Save the world stuff."

I swallowed. *What would you say, Angie? Tell me what you'd say if you knew.* "Not saving it," I said, twisting the phone cord around my thumb. "I don't think anybody can do that 'cause it's already over the edge."

"Yeah," Angie said. "Isn't that messed up?"

We talked for a while longer but it was hard to think of anything except Angie finding out about Mama.

"We should hang out sometimes," Angie said.

"Yeah," I said. "I was gonna call you. Ask you if you wanted to hang out."

"Yeah?" Angie said. "That'd be cool."

After we hung up, I went back into my room and raised the window. It was gray out now, and quiet. Sitting down on the window ledge, I looked up at the cloudy sky. *The amphibians are vanishing,* I kept thinking. Angie. Angie. Angie. I felt like throwing up. I wanted to kiss her. What would it feel like? What would I feel like? Would we fall in love? Maybe. Maybe it could happen.

"Are you ever going to let me read anything in those notebooks?" Mama had asked. And I should have said, *No!* Maybe, *Hell, no!* I should have said, *These are the only things I have that are mine, all mine. The only things I have that won't mess my life up by being gay. The only things that won't stop calling me if they find out.*

Angie. Angie. Angie. I didn't want to hope too much. She was going to find out some way sooner or later. But she had called me. And she hadn't laughed when I told her about the amphibians. Maybe, I couldn't help thinking. Maybe.

I picked up the phone and dialed. She answered after the first ring.

"Angie," I said. "Maybe we could hang out now."

Chapter Fourteen

IT WAS RAINING AGAIN and cold, so the park was empty. Angie pulled her jacket closed, over those breasts, hiding those breasts. I remembered something stupid Mama had said — *It's okay to be nice to women* — so I wiped the bench dry with my jacket before we sat down. Angie moved closer to me. So close, our shoulders were touching. Then I was shivering. Not from the cold but from something — shivering from the inside out. We didn't say anything for a long time. Watching the rain. Watching the empty park. Trying hard not to look at each other.

"I always thought you were cool, Mel," Angie said.

"Yeah," I said, kind of glancing at her but

mostly looking straight ahead. Sitting on my hands and looking straight ahead. "I thought that about you." I tried to sound calm, but the words came out shaky, like they were barely on the tip of something in the back of my throat. I know it sounds like a lie, but I leaned over and kissed her then, quick so that I wouldn't be thinking about it. So fast my teeth bumped her lips. *Stupid, stupid me.*

Angie laughed. She closed her eyes when she laughed and I had never seen anybody laugh like that. It made me smile, from someplace deep that I had forgotten about.

"You never kissed anybody before?"

"I kissed lots of people," I said, sitting up straighter, looking off.

"No you haven't," Angie said. When I glanced at her again she was looking at me, straight on. She knew I was lying.

"I been kissing girls since I was ten," I said.

"Lie number two," Angie said, laughing.

I swallowed. *No Angie. Lie number three. There's another one. Bigger and worse.*

We didn't say anything for a long time, looking off, watching the drizzle, slick against gray-black ground. Rain dripped from the hoops. I thought of the hollow bounce of a basketball and the sound repeated itself in my head — over and over. And the silence filled us up.

"I don't have a lot of friends," Angie said quietly, after a long time had passed. "You mad at me for teasing you?"

I shook my head. "It's nothing." I felt lame making her think I was mad.

"Sometimes I don't know the right things to say," Angie said. She wiped her chin with the back of her hand. "I talk to myself a lot. You don't have to worry about saying the wrong things to yourself." She smiled a little bit, the corners of her mouth turning up, but nothing else about her face changed. I wanted to hold her hand. I wanted to know what it would feel like to have her fingers against my palm. "I'm kind of to myself mostly," she said. "It's better that way."

I nodded, taking my hands from beneath my legs and staring at them. I can palm a basketball, almost. Ralphy says it's about control and muscle. Maybe I had weak hands.

If I was a real liar I would say I took Angie's hand then, that I leaned over and kissed her again. But it didn't happen that way. She kissed *me*. Maybe that was okay because only for a little while did I think about Mama and Kristin kissing and then, after that, it was Angie, all Angie. Beautiful, beautiful Angie.

We kissed for a long time. When we stopped, we just sat there, a little bit embarrassed. It was like all of the words went out of us. Maybe we didn't need any right then.

The rain had started coming down harder, but it didn't seem as though Angie was in any hurry to get out of it. Something about her sitting there, like nothing mattered, like it wasn't even raining, made me want to tell her everything. But I just shivered and continued looking straight ahead.

"I don't have a lot going on," I said. "I, you know, collect my stamps and watch some TV and write . . ."

"Poetry?"

I shook my head.

"I write some poetry sometimes," she said softly. "Stuff about life and my family." When I looked at her, she was smiling. Looking at me and smiling.

"What's your family like?" Maybe she had a dyke mother, too. Maybe this was the perfect ending.

"Mother, father, sister, sister, brother, brother,

brother," Angie was saying. I felt myself closing up, switching off — like a light with a dimmer switch. She would run screaming if she knew. Screaming, screaming, back to her big, big family. Back to her normal life.

Chapter Fifteen

TOWARD THE MIDDLE of August, it got cold
suddenly, and me and Sean and Ralphy
ended up walking the neighborhood with heavy
dungaree jackets hanging like capes from our
heads. Ralph said seasons changing depressed
the hell out of him. Sean was quiet, too quiet,
and Ralph and I kept nudging him with our
elbows trying to get him to say something.

We finally gave up and the three of us fell
silent for about four blocks. When we passed
Angie, I smiled at her.

"Hey," I said.

"Hey yourself," Angie said back, falling in
step with us.

I hadn't called her since that day in the park.
Maybe she thought I didn't like her.

"Rasta woman," Ralph said.

Angie rolled her eyes at Ralph. "Stupid. *You're* the one with locks."

"Who you calling stupid?" Ralph raised one eyebrow.

"I'm calling you stupid," Angie said over her shoulder.

"Leave her alone, Ralph," I said.

Ralph was frowning. "She's trying to be cute in front of you. I'll show her who's stupid."

"Yeah," I said. "Whatever."

Angie and I walked bumping shoulders. Ralph and Sean gave us glances, but didn't say anything. Sean was glaring. Maybe he was jealous.

I took my jacket off my head and put it on. It was too big. Everything we owned was too big. *"You planning on doing a lot of growing?"* Mama asked last time she took me shopping.

"It's the style," I told her but she just pulled her lips to the side of her face and paid for everything.

Now I pulled the pants up a bit and stole a look at Angie. I could tell she was still mad from Ralphy messing with her.

"Don't listen to him," I said softly.

"Oh, I'm not even hearing it," Angie said.

We walked along silently for a while, Ralphy and Sean a few paces behind us.

"I guess we should double-date sometimes, huh?" Ralphy said. I knew this was his way of apologizing, so I winked at him. Angie smiled and said she guessed it would be fun.

"Yeah," Sean said. "Why don't you take her out on a double date with your mama and that dyke she's seeing."

I turned. *Please, God. Please let me be imagining this.*

"Don't look at me like I'm crazy," he said. "Everybody knows."

"Knows what?" Ralph was asking but I didn't wait to hear Sean's answer before I swung hard and landed a punch across his jaw. Something snapped and Sean seemed to move toward me in slow motion. I caught him around the neck, feeling my fist connect with his nose. Someone was trying to pull us apart and in the distance I could hear Angie telling me to stop. Sean's knee landed hard in my stomach and I felt myself falling backwards.

"Stop it," Ralph was saying. Someone was pulling Sean off of me. I kicked into the air and connected.

Pancho, the guy who owned the store we were standing in front of, was holding Sean's arms, but Sean was struggling against him.

"Your mother's a dyke," Sean yelled. *Angie,* I kept thinking, looking around for her. She was standing in front of the store, where a small group had gathered. She looked confused and angry. Now she knew. Now everyone in the whole stupid world knew.

"Stop talking junk," Ralph said.

I swallowed, breathing hard to keep from crying.

"No fighting here," Pancho was saying. "You want to fight, go back where you live."

"Don't worry, Pancho," Ralph said. "They won't be throwing down anymore." He looked around at the crowd. "Did someone die?" he asked sarcastically, and reluctantly, the group began to scatter. "Man. This is one nosey hood."

Pancho disappeared back inside his store and Ralph loosened his grip on me but didn't let go.

"I've seen her with that white lady," Sean said. "I saw them sitting in her car last night. Your mama touching her like they were in love or something." He spit. Someone else said something, but I couldn't hear anything anymore.

I was backing away, then I was turning and running fast and hard as hell away from there. Away from everyone. *I hated her. I hated her.*

EC

What is this? What makes life so crazy? How come it's her of all the mothers in the world that has to be a dyke? How come it can't be Ralph's mom? Or Sean's? Or even Angie's?

Chapter Sixteen

I T STARTED RAINING AGAIN Monday night and didn't stop. Tuesday and Wednesday came and went without a word from Sean or Ralph — or Angie. On Thursday morning, when I pushed the plants apart to look out the living room window, I could see Mrs. Shirley was back, her damp-looking pillow propped on the sill, a yellow rain slicker draped over her head and shoulders. *Once,* I kept thinking, *I had a life and friends, and a girlfriend named Angie. But that was a long time ago, maybe in a dream.*

Two little girls walked up the block, wearing matching Mickey Mouse raincoats. Mrs. Shirley waved and the girls waved back, then linked arms and skipped around the corner.

At seven, Mama came home and started cooking silently. Three times, since my fight with Sean, she had tried to talk to me, and three times, I had turned away from her, mumbling, "Nothing. Just leave me alone." Now, she was finally listening.

Every night this week, the minute I heard her footsteps on the stairs, I retreated to my room and put on my Walkman. Tonight, when she came in, I was listening to Arrested Development do their version of that song "Everyday People," and drawing pictures of breasts in one of my notebooks.

Mama stuck her head in and said something, but the music was up so loud, it seemed like her lips were moving without making any sound. I was sitting on my bed with my back against the wall. When her lips moved like that, I felt my chest go hollow. Something about her being so quiet made me think of death and for the first time I wondered what it would mean if she died.

No father. No mother. No Ralph. No Sean. No Angie. And it was all *her* fault, but now I couldn't even blame her because she was all I had.

I pulled one of the earphones away from my head.

"You want green beans or peas?" Mama asked.

Dropping the earphone back against my ear, I mumbled that it didn't matter and Mama went back into the kitchen.

If she died, I'd be alone.

I stared at my bare feet. The two smallest toes on the left one curled, the smallest one over the next one. Mama said these were her toes and once she showed me, pulling off her shoe so I could see where hers curled in the exact same way. Like twins. What if I *was* just like her? Even if Angie's kiss had given me butter-flies and made me so hard. . . .

These were *my* toes! Me, Melanin Sun, the part of me that didn't have a single thing to do with any bit of her! Or Kristin. It was *them* and *me*. And if she died, our little bit of family would be gone. So we had to hold on to the little bit and maybe stretch it, even if holding on to blood meant losing friends. If she died, I would be the only thing left of us. Me and my stupid, stupid notebooks.

I would be like the beginning of some-thing — but not really, because I'd also be the end with no connection to a past. Like a third-

generation slave with no known relatives. I'd
be in an in-between world.

Mama came back in. Her lips mouthed *Dinner's ready* and I shrugged again. "I'll eat later,"
I said.

She snapped off the stereo and I took the
headphones off.

"You'll eat now," she said, standing there
with her arms folded.

"I'm not hungry *now*."

"Well, then, you'll sit down with me while
I eat."

I rolled my eyes. "I don't want to look at
you."

Now she was frowning, looking past me, out
the window.

"Maybe I've had enough of this. I'm sick of
you sulking around this house. I'm sick of the
faces, the disrespect. . . ."

"Oh, like you respect me."

Mama looked at me. "May I finish?"

"I'm not stopping you."

"Kristin's going to be around a while, so we
might as well start dealing, Mel. I'm sorry if
this hurts, if it's hard, but it *is*, and that's the
jump-off point."

"What, EC? You want me to just say, 'Okay,

my mama's a dyke and everything's perfect'?"

Mama raised her eyebrows. "Yes. Basically, that's what I want."

I looked at her like she was crazy. "No! It doesn't *work like that*. Who do you think I am, God?"

"I think you're the Melanin Sun I raised to be tolerant."

"I am tolerant. Of everybody else. But here, on this block where everybody knows everybody's business, I don't want to have to fight and dodge people and lie to live."

"Who are you fighting?" she asked. When I didn't say anything, she said, "Ralph and Sean?"

I pressed my lips together and stared out the window.

Mama exhaled. "So they know." She leaned back, her arms still folded, and softly hit the back of her head a couple of times against the wall.

"Everybody knows."

"Is that why you're not leaving the house?" she asked quietly.

I nodded.

"You can't stay inside forever, Mel," Mama said gently.

I stretched my hands out, palms up, and stud-
ied the tiny lines in them. "They think you're
a freak."

Mama sighed. "I don't care what *they* think.
I want to know what *you* think."

I looked at her. "How come it has to be her?"

"I love her."

"How come you can't just love a man like
everybody else? Even a white man if you had
to."

"Not everybody else loves men, Melanin
Sun. . . ."

"Like *most* people," I said.

"Because I'm not most people."

"Do you hate *me*, EC?"

Mama shook her head. "Of course not, M.
You're the closest person in the world to me."

"But you don't like men."

"I never said I didn't like them. I'm just not
romantically *attracted* to them."

"But what about my father?"

"I was young."

"And what about the other guys you dated?"

"*You* hated all of them," Mama smiled.

"But weren't you attracted to any of them?"

Mama thought for a moment. "Yeah. Some,

I guess. But it's nothing like what I feel for Kristin."

"Is it 'cause she's white?"

Mama looked at me. "No and yes, sometimes. It's complicated."

"It *is*, isn't it?" I scowled. EC was so . . . so . . . stupid.

"I like the contrast of us, the differences between us — and I like the way we've found our way to each other across color lines. Kristin's amazing to me. I like *her* — everything about her, and her whiteness is a part of her." Mama said. "Does that make sense?"

"No!"

"I didn't think it would. Look, honey, this may sound lame, but I'd like to ask you for a favor. The next time Kristin is here, I want you to try to get to know her. See us together as people. I'm still EC. She's Kristin. That's all I'm asking of you."

I started to say something, but Mama cut me off.

"Just try, Melanin Sun. I need you to do that. Can you?"

I shook my head no.

"Can you just do it for me, M?"

I shook my head.

Mama thought a moment. "Who am I, Mel?"

"EC," I mumbled.

"No. Who am I?"

"Mama."

"Do you love me?"

"I have to," I said.

"No you don't. You don't have to do any-thing. Do you love me?"

I nodded.

"Can you not hate me for one day? Can you love me like you used to for a day, Mel?"

"I do love you. I just hate Kristin."

"But you don't know her."

"I hate the *idea* of her, Mama. You know what I mean. Why does she have to be with you? I wish she was dead. I wish she wasn't ever born."

Mama frowned. "Well, I don't." She shrugged.

"You hate me, don't you?"

Mama put her hand on her hip. "What makes you think I can't love both of you?"

" 'Cause she's white and I'm black. 'Cause she's a lady and I'm not! Don't be stupid. You know why."

Mama sighed. "Just see her as human, Mel.

Just walk into one day without being so mad at me."

"And how do I have to walk out of it?"

Mama lifted her hands. "However you walk out of it."

"What kind of day?"

"Breakfast, maybe a trip to the beach or a picnic in Prospect Park. Dinner out somewhere."

"And if I walk away hating her as much as I do right now, will you stop seeing her?"

Mama shook her head. "No, but I won't bring her here anymore."

I thought of Ralph and Sean. I thought of Angie. "Deal," I said.

"Deal," Mama repeated. "Now, since this may be the last time we sit down together as friends, can I have my last meal with you?"

Reluctantly, I smiled and closed my notebook. "Yeah," I said. "For old time's sake."

Chapter Seventeen

WHEN I THOUGHT I had finally gotten him and Sean out of my head, Ralph called. I was so surprised to hear his voice on the other end asking about my mother, I stuttered when I told him that she was at the library, studying. Then everything came right back and I felt myself getting mad all over again.

"For who?" Ralph nosed, as though it hadn't been almost two weeks since we'd last spoken.

"For herself. What did you call for?"

"For what?" Ralph said, ignoring my question.

"What are you calling for?" I asked again. He had deserted me. Had left me hanging after all of these years of being homeboys. And now he thought he could just call up and say hey.

There was a pause. After a moment, Ralph said, "I was wondering what you were up to, that's all."

"Nothing."

More silence. I cradled the receiver between my shoulder and ear while I doodled on a pad Mama had mounted on the wall beside the phone.

"You want to hang later, maybe rent a video?"

I looked behind me at the clock above the kitchen window. It was a little after four. *Video Music Box* came on at four-thirty.

"I was watching TV." The television was still on in the living room with its volume turned all the way down.

"Oh."

"How's Sean?"

"His eye is still pretty messed up, but he's okay, I guess."

"That's good."

"What were you going to watch?"

"*Video Music Box.*"

"Yeah," Ralph said, as though I had asked him a question.

"Sean say anything else about my mother?"

"Nah. He didn't really have nothing else to say. His mom said he had to stay away from you, though."

"Oh. I don't care." But I did care. It hurt. It hurt worse than anything.

"EC still . . . ?"

"Yeah . . . Kristin."

"Oh," Ralphael said. "It's no big deal, you know. Like what goes on with your mother doesn't have to do with anybody else, right?"

"Yeah, I know. I mean . . . thanks." I swallowed and bit my bottom lip. "Everybody knows, right?"

"Probably. You know how this block is."

We didn't say anything for a moment. Then Ralph laughed. "You know what my moms said?"

"What?"

"She said she saw EC day before yesterday and she looked happier than anything. Mama said she should go out and find herself a woman if that's what it's all about."

I laughed.

"But not everybody's saying stuff like that."

"I don't care," I said.

"Me either."

"What else you hear?"

"Nothing . . ." Ralph was hesitant.

"You lie."

"Mrs. Shirley said . . ."

"What, Ralph?"

"She said someone should call the authorities on EC and take you out of that house 'cause . . . she's . . . she said your mother's . . . unfit."

"Unfit for what?" I asked. My voice got high suddenly. What the hell was she talking about?

"To be your mother."

"Oh, she's full of it. Anyway, I wouldn't let anybody take me anyplace. She's still my mom. Mrs. Shirley should take her fat behind out of that window and do something with her own life."

"Mrs. Shirley's stupid," I heard Ralph say, but I wasn't listening anymore. I was thinking about Mama and tomorrow when we were supposed to spend the day with Kristin. What if they came for me before then? What if the authorities came tonight and slipped me away from here and made new rules?

"Mel," Ralph was saying, "I don't care what people say. If anything, they should come take Mrs. Shirley away for spending the whole day in the window instead of looking after her own kids."

"They wouldn't, though," I said.

Ralph sniffed. "I got a cold from all that rain, and Mama's not letting me hear the end of it." He went into a coughing spasm. When he spoke again, his voice was broken up, like there was something stuck in the back of his throat. "If you want to hang sometimes, give me a call. We only got a few more days of summer vacation, anyway. Might as well use it up."

"Yeah," I said. "We might as well."

Sean

It ends like this between us, without apology — like a fatal sickness in the night, like fire sweeping through, like the last blank page at the end of a book, as if the story had never been.

Maybe when we get older, people will forget this all and ask me, "Whatever happened to your homeboy, Sean?" and I'll have to say I don't know because I don't, and I probably never will. So it ends like this.

Chapter Eighteen

NO ONE CAME IN THE NIGHT to take me away. Mama woke me early the next morning — so early the sky was just beginning to break with the first rays of daylight. I thought maybe she was losing her mind to be shaking me awake at the crack of dawn.

The apartment was cool and bathed in a pretty purplish light. Someone was in the kitchen banging pots around. On my way to the bathroom, I peeked in and saw Kristin there, dressed in a pair of Mama's shorts and a T-shirt, turning down the flame underneath the teakettle.

Last night, Mama had come in alone. But later on, I thought I dreamed that the bell rang and Mama called *I'll throw the keys down*. I hate that fake reality that sometimes exists between sleep and wake. It obscures things. Once, right after Mama told me about her and Kristin, I had a dream that I was living in a house in Connecticut with a man Mama had just married. I woke up waiting for this guy to wake me up to take me shopping and I must have sat on the edge of my bed for a good half hour waiting for him to walk into my room.

"Morning, Melanin Sun," Kristin said, too brightly for this hour. Too brightly for anything. But today was the day and after it was all over, I wouldn't have to deal with her anymore so I mumbled something that might have passed for good morning.

"So you're not a morning person, huh?" Kristin lifted her glasses and rubbed her eyes. She was still smiling. There was something about her — a mellow something. It put me off a bit.

As I stepped out of the shower, I could hear Mama singing softly in the kitchen *Oh happy day . . . When Jesus washed. When He washed. He washed my sins away*.

"I made toast and eggs scrambled hard like EC said you like them," Kristin said, putting a plate down in front of me. "And grits." She smiled. I guess Mama had been giving her some soul food lessons. I looked over at Mama sitting across from me, wondering what she was getting from Kristin in return. Kristin brought two more plates to the table and sat in the seat between us.

The grits were lumpy but I ate them anyway, stirring my eggs into them and scooping it all up with my toast.

Kristin picked at her food, doing that eating-everything-separately thing again. She spread a tiny bit of jelly on her toast and took a small bite.

"So," she said, pushing her glasses up on her nose. "Anybody want to hear a joke?"

I chewed silently, without looking up.

Mama must have nodded, because she continued.

"A piece of string walks into a bar and the bartender says, 'We don't serve string . . .' "

"Frayed knot," I said.

"Guess you heard it already, huh?"

I looked at Kristin. She looked a little tired and for a moment, I was sorry I had cut in on her joke. "About a hundred years ago."

"Funny," Kristin smiled. "You don't look that old."

Mama laughed. Kristin had caught me off

guard, so I smiled and stuffed a chunk of toast in my mouth. *This part is easy,* I thought. We three here in the house with no one around wasn't hard at all.

After breakfast, I played Game Boy while Mama and Kristin went about fixing a picnic lunch. Kristin had suggested we go to Prospect Park, but Mama said she felt more like lying near some water so we decided on Jones Beach. They were talking easily now. Kristin had a strange laugh, like a cough almost that rumbled from the back of her throat.

"I didn't bring a bathing suit," Kristin said, heading toward Mama's room.

"Bottom drawer, right side," Mama yelled from the kitchen.

A few minutes later, heading back into the kitchen, Kristin stopped at the foot of my bed and kicked it.

"You hate me?" she asked, smiling.

I shrugged, keeping my eyes on the game. "I don't know you."

She kicked the bed a few more times until I looked at her like she was losing her mind. Maybe she was crazy.

"What do you want to know?" she asked. She had her hands in the pockets of her shorts, and the way she stood — kind of like a gangly white boy — made me want to smile. I had never met a lady, besides Mama, who was so . . . so *relaxed*. I felt the side of my mouth turning up. She stood the way I was always trying to stand, sort of cool and calm and collected. I could almost picture her saying, "No problem."

"Nothing," I said.

"I'll tell you anything."

I could see the outline of Mama's blue bathing suit underneath Kristin's T-shirt. She had small breasts. Her legs were long and kind of tanned. Nice legs, I guess. If you like that. I wondered if Mama had touched them and how.

"How long you been," I stuttered, "you know?"

"Gay?" She smiled and the dimple on her cheek appeared. "G-a-y. You can say it. It's not a four-letter word."

I looked away from her, embarrassed. The way she talked made me think of somebody younger, someone familiar . . .

"Gay," I said.

"Forever," she said, pulling her pale hair up off her shoulders into a ponytail that she twisted into a bun. When she moved her hand, it fell again, sweeping across her shoulder.

"What's forever?" I asked, growing annoyed.

Kristin shrugged and sat down on the edge of my bed.

"As long as I can remember."

"You never had a boyfriend?"

She smiled again, but this time got a faraway look. "A couple. But they were, you know . . ." She looked at me a moment and smirked. "No, I guess you don't know."

I shook my head.

"They weren't my type."

"And Mama's your type?"

Kristin nodded.

"Why?"

"Well, she's smart and beautiful and driven . . ." She eyed me. "You can't see it, huh?"

"How come you two can't just be friends?" I asked, going back to Game Boy.

"Because we like each other more than that."

"More than what?"

"More than *friends*," Kristin said, as though I should know that already.

"What's the big difference?"

Kristin and I looked at each other. She scooted back on the bed until she was sitting right next to me, our backs against the wall. She pulled her knees up and wrapped her arms around her legs. Mama! That's who she reminded me of. The old EC. The one who was fun and playful and laughed a lot. The one who moved like she had been born walking. Kristin moved like that. And talked and laughed a bit like that.

"Okay," she said. "Who's your friend?"

I thought for a moment and told her it was Ralphael.

"Do you like going to the movies with him?"

I nodded.

"And spending time with him?"

I nodded again, not knowing what she was getting at.

"Okay. Now, would you like to *kiss* Ralphael?"

"No!"

She threw her hands up. "That's the difference."

"But you're not *supposed* to want to do that."

"Who says?" Kristin asked.

"It's gross."

"Maybe to you," she said smiling. "Kissing a guy's *gross* to me."

I blinked. Put Game Boy on pause. "Kissing a guy really grosses you out?" I asked, frowning.

"Let's just say it doesn't . . . appeal to me," she said.

I thought about it for a moment. "It grosses EC out, too?"

Kristin shrugged. "I can't speak for her."

Mama came in with the picnic basket slung on her arm.

"Sodas, sandwiches, chips, potato salad, cookies. Anything I forgot?"

"It really grosses you out, Ma? Why?" I asked.

Mama looked puzzled. Kristin was trying not to smile.

"Mel has a question for you, EC."

Chapter Nineteen

AT JONES BEACH, Kristin led us to the area that was mostly gay. It was strange seeing so many of them all coupled up in one place, but it made it feel less weird to be there with Ma and Kristin. If Sean and Ralph had been with me, they probably would have lost it. We passed a group of people that Kristin knew and she stopped and introduced us. I eyed a black man sitting between his white boyfriend's legs. When he looked over at me and smiled, I turned back to Kristin's friends, all white except for one girl who looked a little bit older than me. Later, Kristin told me the girl was the adopted daughter of one of the couples. A part of me wanted to go back and talk to her, ask her if it was as weird for her as it was for me. But another part of me had no desire to be with other gay people. Next thing, I'd have a whole world of them hanging out at my house or something.

We moved down the beach and settled on our blanket about two hundred feet away from Kristin's friends.

"We could've sat with them," EC said, peeling off her T-shirt and shorts. The roll of fat that she had been worried about was long gone. She pulled a pair of sunglasses from her bag, slid them on, and lay back on the blanket.

Kristin gazed out at the water. "Nah," she said. "I wanted quality time."

Mama smiled but didn't say anything. She reached across me, grabbed Kristin's hand, and squeezed it. I swallowed.

The water lapped silently up onto the sand. A few yards away, a group of men were setting up a volleyball game. A black dog ran up to our blanket and sniffed at my sneakers.

"C'mon Magpie," a redheaded woman called and, just as quickly, the dog ran off.

Kristin scooted closer to me, wrapped her arms around her knees, and sighed.

"I'm gonna walk," I said, grabbing my notebook.

"I'll walk with you," Kristin said, jumping up.

I started to say something but didn't. It was a free country.

We walked silently for a while. Kristin kept digging her toes into the sand, then shaking them off.

"I hate sand," she said, "but I love the beach. Isn't that weird?"

I nodded.

"I guess I'm weird," she said. "But it's so beautiful here. I like it in the winter, too. Have you ever been here in the winter?"

I shook my head.

"We should come sometime. Nobody on the beach. It's perfect. Sometimes aloneness is so perfect."

"I wear it like a coat," I said, and Kristin looked at me like she couldn't believe those words had come from my mouth. Then she smiled.

"I hate the cold," I said. "I don't think I could stand the beach in the winter."

"Layers. Lots of layers and you won't even feel it."

I looked out over the water. The waves were

calm today. "I wouldn't come here in the winter," I said.

"Why not?"

"Just wouldn't."

We continued walking.

"I've always wanted a family," Kristin was saying. "I lost mine."

"How?" I asked, still staring at the water. Kristin was talking softly. I wondered if Mama was asleep back on our blanket or nervously waiting for us to return.

"They found out I'm queer," Kristin said, tossing her hair. She looked like a girl then — stubborn and hurt. "They stopped speaking to me. Wrote me off."

"Oh."

Had I written Mama off? She must have been afraid. Afraid that she'd lose me. And all the while I had been afraid, too. Of what everybody would think. And of losing her.

The beach was getting crowded. A group of women put down a blanket a few feet away. One of them smiled at Kristin.

"What about Christmas?" I said after a long time had passed.

Kristin frowned, then shielded her eyes

with her hand and looked out over the water.

"What about it?"

"Who do you do it with?"

"Family."

"But I thought you . . ."

"Not the family I was born into," she said. "The family I made for myself. Close friends." She took her hand away from her eyes. I stopped and took off my sneakers.

"You have EC's feet," Kristin said, staring at my toes.

I curled and uncurled my toes. The sand felt soft and hot against them.

What would Ralphael think if he saw me and Kristin walking along Jones Beach? I guess he didn't really care. At least, that's what he said when he called me. Tomorrow we were planning on going to see a movie or something. He said Sean was down South for the next week before school started. *Maybe,* Ralphael had said, *he'll come back thinking different.* Yeah, I had said, not believing for a minute it would happen, but hoping. Maybe.

"Maybe this Christmas will be different," Kristin was saying. "Maybe we can all go away somewhere. Me, you, EC, and whoever you'd like to bring. That would be nice."

I could bring Ralphy. He's cool about Mama and Kristin. Or maybe I'd bring Angie . . . if she was still speaking to me. If she would want to come. When I looked at Kristin, her eyes were uncertain behind her glasses and filled with something . . . hope. I wanted to ask her what it felt like to have a family still alive somewhere and not be able to talk to them. Did it feel like it did with my father? Hollow and empty sometimes, and sometimes it didn't matter? Or was it like the disappearance of the common toad, just all of a sudden, the last one died and it's like it never ever was?

"Can we sit a minute?"

I nodded and we sat at the edge of the water.

"You miss them?" I asked.

"Yeah," Kristin said. She leaned on her knees so that her chin stuck out a little and she smiled. Her smile was nice, I decided, honest and sad. "Sometimes a lot."

"If you don't have a girlfriend . . . it's kind of just you by yourself?"

She nodded. "I still have my friends . . . but it's lonely." A sandpiper darted past. "Yesterday," Kristin said, "I was thinking about buffalo. Can you imagine being the last to die off?"

I shook my head. "I'd want to go in a crowd."

"Me, too," Kristin said softly. "Me, too."

We sat there without saying anything for a long time. People passing by must have wondered about us — how strange we looked together — a black guy and white woman sitting silently, staring out at the water. But I didn't care anymore what people were thinking. Some part of me was starting to move inside of myself, shutting out all those nosey eyes and nasty things people can think to say.

"If I had to be the last one like myself," I said, "I'd want to run and run. Hard as I could until I couldn't run anymore. Least that way I'd have felt the wind on my face once more before I kicked off."

"And the sun," Kristin said, smiling.

"Yeah," I agreed. "The sun."

Chapter Twenty

SOMETIMES YOU HAVE TO START at the beginning and work your way back. As Kristin and I sat talking, something began melting inside of me. I don't know how to say it, don't know how to write it in my notebooks. But some small closed up space for Kristin started opening, growing, filling itself in. Like an eclipse — the way the moon rushes out to cover up the sun. That moment with Kristin on the beach was like an eclipse — and quick as it had come, the moon pulled away and the sun was back. No one stops to think, though — that maybe there is a reason for the darkness. Maybe people have to be reminded of it — of its power. At night, we go to sleep against the darkness. And if we wake up before morning, a lot of times we're afraid. We need it all though — the darkness and the light. The Melanin and the Sun. Mama and Kristin.

Later on, when we walked back to the blanket, I looked over at Mama. I would be fourteen in a month and a half, and we were both afraid. Groping for some sort of light on the other side of all of this. Something that would guide us somewhere, help us find our way back to each other. We didn't know how any of this would end. But maybe it didn't matter. We had each other. We would always have each other.

When Kristin lay back against Mama's shoulder, I had to look away, tears burning at the edges of my eyes. It wouldn't be easy. All the hate and gossip and fights and maybes. . . .

I looked at Mama. She was squinting up at me and smiling.

"Hey, Mel."

"Hey yourself," I said, trying to smile, walking backwards away from them, toward the water.

I didn't know what would happen tomorrow or the next day or the next. I didn't know what would happen with Ralphy or Kristin or

Angie. . . . I didn't know if it would ever stop mattering what people thought. But I was sure of Mama, sure of my notebooks. And for the quickest moment, walking backwards against the sun, I was sure of me.

Maybe that's all that matters.

ABOUT THE AUTHOR

JACQUELINE WOODSON is the author of many
fine novels for children and young adults, including *I Hadn't Meant to Tell You This*; *Last
Summer with Maizon*; *Maizon at Blue Hill*, which
was an ALA Best Book for Young Adults; and
The Dear One. She is on the faculty of the
Goddard College MFA Writing Program and
is the recipient of the *Kenyon Review* Award
for Literary Excellence in Fiction. She was born
in Ohio and grew up in Greenville, South
Carolina, and in Brooklyn, New York, where
she currently lives.